The Notorious Wolfes

A powerful dynasty, where secrets and scandal never sleep!

THE DYNASTY

Eight siblings, blessed with wealth, but denied the one thing they wanted—a father's love.
A family destroyed by one man's thirst for power.

THE SECRET

Haunted by their past and driven to succeed, the Wolfes scattered to the far corners of the globe. But secrets never sleep and scandal is starting to stir….

THE POWER

Now, the Wolfe brothers are back, stronger than ever, but hiding hearts as hard as granite.
It's said that even the blackest of souls can be healed by the purest of love…
But can the dynasty rise again?

Each month, Harlequin Presents is delighted to bring you an exciting new installment from The Notorious Wolfes. You won't want to miss out!

A NIGHT OF SCANDAL—*Sarah Morgan*
THE DISGRACED PLAYBOY—*Caitlin Crews*
THE STOLEN BRIDE—*Abby Green*
THE FEARLESS MAVERICK—*Robyn Grady*
THE MAN WITH THE MONEY—*Lynn Raye Harris*
THE TROPHY WIFE—*Janette Kenny*
THE GIRL THAT LOVE FORGOT—*Jennie Lucas*
THE LONE WOLFE—*Kate Hewitt*

8 volumes to collect and treasure!

"Sorry—I'm just not used to having a movie star in my living room. It feels—"

"How does it feel?" The way he was looking at her turned her insides to liquid. His eyes slid to her mouth and Katie felt the blood pound through her veins. Being the focus of his attention was the most heady, exciting thing that had ever happened to her. He was looking at her as if, as if—

Oh, God, Nathaniel Wolfe was going to kiss her—

Why, oh, why hadn't she stuck to her diet?

Wound tight with sexual awareness, she swayed toward him. She saw him lower his head toward hers and then he gave a sharp frown and turned away abruptly, walking to the far side of the room.

Katie stood like an idiot, completely thrown off balance. What had she expected? Nathaniel Wolfe was a superstar. What on earth had made her think he'd want to kiss someone like her? Clearly she was delusional.

Sarah Morgan

A NIGHT OF SCANDAL

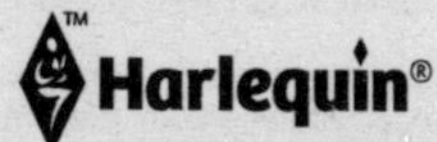

TORONTO NEW YORK LONDON
AMSTERDAM PARIS SYDNEY HAMBURG
STOCKHOLM ATHENS TOKYO MILAN MADRID
PRAGUE WARSAW BUDAPEST AUCKLAND

ISBN-13: 978-0-373-13000-9

A NIGHT OF SCANDAL
First published in the U.K. as THE TORTURED RAKE

First North American Publication 2011

Special thanks and acknowledgment are given to Sarah Morgan for her contribution to The Notorious Wolfes series

This edition published by arrangement with Harlequin Books S.A.

For questions and comments about the quality of this book please contact us at Customer_eCare@Harlequin.ca.

www.Harlequin.com

Printed in U.S.A.

All about the author...
Sarah Morgan

USA **TODAY** bestselling author **SARAH MORGAN** writes lively, sexy stories for both the Harlequin Presents and Medical Romance lines.

As a child, Sarah dreamed of being a writer and although she took a few interesting detours on the way, she is now living that dream. With her writing career, she has successfully combined business with pleasure and she firmly believes that reading romance is one of the most satisfying and fat-free escapist pleasures available. Her stories are unashamedly optimistic and she is always pleased when she receives letters from readers saying that her books have helped them through hard times.

RT Book Reviews has described her writing as "action packed and sexy" and nominated her books for their Reviewer's Choice Award and their "Top Pick" slot.

Sarah lives near London with her husband and two children, who innocently provide an endless supply of authentic dialogue. When she isn't writing or reading, Sarah enjoys music, movies and any activity that takes her outdoors.

Readers can find out more about Sarah and her books from her website www.sarahmorgan.com. She can also be found on Facebook and Twitter.

To my fellow "Wolfe" authors—Caitlin, Abby, Robyn, Lynn, Jeanette, Jennie and Kate. Working on this series with you was so much fun. You're a fantastic, talented bunch of women and I can't wait to read the final stories!

CHAPTER ONE

THEY were waiting for him to fail.

Nathaniel Wolfe, bad boy of Hollywood and focus of millions of women's erotic fantasies, stood alone in the wings of the famous London theatre, listening to the excited hum of conversation from the waiting audience.

He knew they could roughly be divided into two camps. Women who had come to see if his face and body lived up to the promise of the big screen and men who had come to see whether he could really act.

The knives had been out for him since it had been announced that he would play the title role in a modern interpretation of Shakespeare's *Richard II*.

They thought he couldn't do it. They thought that the awards, the plaudits, the box office successes were all a result of clever camera work and a handsome face. They thought he had no talent.

A cynical smile tugged at the corners of his mouth.

He was going to blast their prejudices into the stratosphere. By tomorrow morning no one would be questioning his talent. The headlines wouldn't be *Can the Big Bad Wolfe Really Act?* but *Big Bad Wolfe Silences Critics with Outstanding Performance*. He was going to show them an emotional range that had never before been seen in the theatre.

The director was hovering in the wings and they shared a

single brief glance. It had been a stormy collaboration with Nathaniel insisting on playing the part the way he wanted to do it and the director fighting back. Between them they'd produced magic that both knew would go down in theatre history.

As the moment approached, Nathaniel closed his eyes and blocked out the outside world. It was the ritual he always used. Within moments, Nathaniel Wolfe ceased to exist.

He was Richard, King of England.

This was what he did. He turned a role into reality. He didn't just act that character, he *became* that character. At the age of nine he'd discovered it was possible to slip into someone else's skin and hide there. It had been a way of escaping from the dark that had licked around the edges of his life. He could be whoever he wanted to be. A knight, a ninja, a dragon slayer, a vampire, a superhero. Desperate, he'd given himself the strength and power to fight back. *To protect those he loved.* Acting had begun as an escape and quickly become a disguise. And that was how he lived his life. Alone and in disguise, depending on no one.

He had no trouble being someone else.

It was being Nathaniel Wolfe that gave him problems.

'The dress does *not* make you look fat.' Katie tightened the corset over rolls of flesh. 'The colour is really flattering, I think you look great. And anyway, you're the Duchess of Gloucester. You're supposed to look—' She broke off as the actress glowered at her. 'Statesman-like,' she finished. 'You're supposed to have gravitas.'

'So you're basically saying I look fat and *old*?'

'No! I picked the costume really carefully.' Realising how that could be interpreted, Katie braced herself for more abuse. 'You're playing the part of a grieving widow so you're not supposed to look bright and cheerful.'

'Are you trying to tell me how to act?'

'No. I'm telling you that you look perfect for the part. *Please* try and relax.'

'How can I relax when I'm cast alongside Nathaniel Wolfe? He is sarcastic, cutting, moody… Yesterday when I made that one simple mistake—'

'He just looked at you,' Katie said soothingly. 'He didn't actually say anything.'

'You don't know how much can be conveyed by the eyes, especially when those eyes belong to Nathaniel Wolfe. When he looks at you it's like being zapped by a laser.' Increasingly agitated, the older woman waved her hand towards the door. 'Go. I need to be around people who understand my temperament.'

Crabby and irritable? 'I still have to zip up your dress.' Katie discovered that her hands were shaking. 'Look, we're all stressed—'

'What do *you* have to be stressed about?'

'Well…' For a moment Katie almost told her about the meeting she had with a top British costume designer and how much was riding on it. She almost blurted out that her debts were so scarily huge she spent her nights creating mental spreadsheets, trying to find a way of paying everything she owed. But if all went well tomorrow, then that would change. This was her big break.

Misinterpreting her silence, the actress made an impatient sound in her throat. 'You have no idea what it's like acting opposite a Hollywood star. You have no idea how it feels to know that every single person in that audience has come to see *him.*' She turned the full force of her wrath onto Katie. 'My dress could split and everyone would still be looking at him! I could be naked and no one would notice!'

Horrified by that thought, Katie took several deep breaths. 'Please calm down. It's just opening-night nerves. Everyone feels the same.'

'Everyone except Nathaniel Wolfe,' the actress snapped.

'He's as remote as Antarctica and every bit as icy. No one dares get too close in case they injure themselves on all that ice.'

'And then they'd sink like the *Titanic.*'

'Are you saying I look like the *Titanic*?'

'No!' Katie decided it was safer not to indulge in conversation. 'You look gorgeous and the dress fits perfectly.'

'Not for much longer. When I'm stressed I just want to eat. And acting alongside Nathaniel Wolfe stresses me. You're young and pretty. Why aren't you backstage wearing a push-up bra and a plunge top like all the other girls?'

'I look ridiculous in a push-up bra and I'd die on the spot if Nathaniel Wolfe actually noticed me. Fortunately he doesn't know I exist. He calls me "wardrobe." Even when I was fitting him for his costume he didn't talk to me. He was on the phone the whole time. Breathe in…' Katie struggled with the zip, praying that it would hold. She didn't want to be the one to point out that eating a truckload of doughnuts between costume fitting and opening night wasn't helpful. 'Nathaniel Wolfe is so famous I find it impossible to act normally around him. When he walks into the room my stomach churns, my mouth falls open and I stare like an idiot, which is *not* a good look. And anyway, he is the ultimate bad boy and I prefer men who are a little less scary.' She fastened the hooks at the neckline. 'There. You're ready. Good luck.'

'It's bad luck to wish an actress good luck. You're supposed to say "break a leg" or something similar.'

Katie sighed. *Break a zip?* 'I'm in charge of wardrobe, if anyone breaks anything it will be a problem because none of the costumes will fit over a plaster cast. And now I have to go and check on John of Gaunt.'

She escaped to the wardrobe department where her close friend and assistant, Claire, was munching a bar of chocolate and reading a celebrity magazine hidden underneath a costume. She glanced up guiltily as Katie entered the room.

'Oops. You caught me peeking into other people's lives—all for the purposes of research, of course.' Her grin turned to a frown as she looked at Katie's face. 'I'm guessing you've just come from sorting out the Duchess of Grizzly Ghastly Gloucester. Did she fit into her dress?'

'Just.' Katie flopped into a chair. Pain stabbed behind her eyes. 'Dressing her in deep purple is great for the character she's playing, but dark colours are very unforgiving against exposed flesh and I have a horrible feeling that her dress is going to split. Do we have any headache pills left?'

'I just swallowed the last. And talking of headaches…' Claire passed her the magazine. 'I don't know if you're going to want to see this, but there's a huge feature on your sister in here. *Is Paula Preston the Most Beautiful Woman in the World?* Well, duh—no, she's the most *airbrushed* woman in the world. How come you're Field and she's Preston? Why don't the two of you have the same surname?'

'She doesn't want anyone to make the connection. She likes to pretend her family doesn't exist.' Katie stared at the picture of her sister and then thought about how much their mother was struggling. Part of her just wanted to get on the phone and yell. She wanted to remind Paula about family loyalty and priorities. But she knew there was no point. 'When it all came out about Dad's gambling problem, she was horrified. I was horrified, too, obviously, but Paula was just so *angry* with Mum for forgiving him and staying with him all those years. She blames her for the fact we had no money when we were growing up and says that if Mum loses the house now, then it's her own fault. She doesn't see why she should pay for what she sees as Mum's weakness.'

'Nice.'

'Sometimes I can't even believe we're related.' Katie chewed the corner of her fingernail and then caught sight of her sister's perfect nails and let her hand drop into her lap. 'It was all too grubby for her. She's created this perfect image for herself and she doesn't want it tarnished by Dad's sins.'

Claire snatched the magazine back from her and ripped out the offending article. 'There.' She scrunched up the pages and threw them in the bin. 'She's where she deserves to be. And now I'm going to watch the wicked Wolfe onstage. It's a once-in-a-lifetime thing. Are you coming?'

'No. I need to look at my drawings again and go over the script before tomorrow.'

'You'll never be able to work in Hollywood if you're star-struck.'

'I'm not star-struck.'

'Yes, you are. When you took his inside leg measurement, your face was like a tomato.'

'OK, maybe I'm Nathaniel Wolfe-struck.'

'The guy is smoking hot, that's for sure.'

Katie twisted the cap off a bottle of water. 'Yes, but he isn't *real*. How well can you ever really know an actor? How do you know when they're acting?' She sipped her water. She knew only too well how easy it was to think you knew someone and then discover you didn't. 'I mean, if Nathaniel Wolfe ever said "I love you" to you, are you seriously going to believe him?'

'I overheard him telling the director that *love* is a four-letter word and he never uses four-letter words. Do you know that the tickets for this sold out in four minutes? *Four minutes.* Incredible. Particularly when you think that Shakespeare is gobbledegook to lots of people. Macbeth talking to skulls—'

'Hamlet.' Katie slipped off her shoes and flexed her toes. 'It was Hamlet.'

'Whatever. I was rubbish at English at school. I used to think Chaucer was something you rested your teacup on.'

'That's saucer, not Chaucer.'

'My point exactly. Anyway, what I'm saying is that he could

be reading his tax return and it would still be a full house. This is Nathaniel Wolfe we're talking about. The man has won every award going, except the Sapphire Screen Award. That's the big one.' Katie thought about the massive hype that surrounded the most prestigious film award in the world. 'He's been nominated three times.'

'I guess it's every actor's ultimate goal. He certainly deserves it this time round.' Claire looked dreamy.

'Even when he's spouting Shakespeare and I don't understand a word he's saying, I still can't stop listening.'

'That's what I'm trying to tell you—it's mind control. It's the voice. And those incredible blue eyes.'

'Can you imagine what it would be like to actually have sex with him? I wonder if you'd stare with your mouth open all the way through?'

'That's one question I'm never going to be able to answer. He doesn't even know I'm alive. Thank goodness.' Katie put the top back on her water and returned the bottle to her bag. 'Listen, about tonight—'

'You are not backing out, so don't even think about it. It starts at eleven and we need to look really sexy. Wear something that shows your cleavage.'

'No way. I still have no idea how I let you talk me into speed dating.'

'You're gorgeous, Katie. You only think you're fat because your sister is Paula Preston, supermodel.'

'I feel so unfit. When this play is over I'm going to be more disciplined about exercise. I want to be toned and sleek. It's depressing watching Nathaniel Wolfe. His body is packed muscle.' Gloomy, Katie flexed her biceps. 'I barely have the strength to lift my water bottle.'

'He looks deadly in that leather jacket you picked out for him. You are utterly amazing at knowing exactly which costume will work best.'

'The costume is supposed to mimic the character's

emotional journey.' Katie glanced down at her ripped jeans. 'I dread to think what my clothes say about my emotional journey but I definitely travelled economy.'

'Your clothes say that you're an overworked, underpaid costume designer with no time to worry about your own wardrobe.'

'And with huge debts.'

'You're incredibly talented. One day someone is going to discover you.'

'Well, I wish someone would discover me quickly.' Panic streaked through her. 'The house sucks everything I earn. It's like a monster.'

'You have to tell your Mum how much you're struggling. She doesn't really need three bedrooms, does she?'

'It's the home she lived in with Dad. It's full of memories.' Emotionally and physically exhausted, Katie closed her eyes. 'Every time I go there she tells me that living in the house is the only thing keeping her going since we lost him. Despite everything, theirs was such an incredible love story. Anyway, if I get this job it will all be fine. Another step up the ladder.'

'I bet your sister would be interested if she knew you were working with Nathaniel Wolfe.' Claire stretched out her legs. 'Do you prefer him in *Alpha Man* or *Dare or Die*?'

'Alpha Man.'

'Seriously?' Claire frowned. '*Alpha Man* was about a Special Forces soldier. I didn't think it would be your sort of thing.'

'I loved the fact he thought he had no heart and then when he met the daughter of his enemy—' Katie's eyes misted '—that bit at the end when he sacrifices himself to save her. I cried for days. I must have watched it a hundred times. Nathaniel Wolfe was crazily good in that movie. And totally gorgeous. If they awarded a Sapphire for Best Physique, he'd win.'

'Talking of the Sapphires—' Claire threw her the magazine '—flick through the rest of that when you get a minute. There's an article on dressing for the big night. They're predicting who will wear what at the ceremony in two weeks' time. You might be interested.'

'Why? I'm never going to be invited to the Sapphire ceremony, which is just as well because I don't think you're allowed to wear holey jeans.' Katie slipped the magazine into her bag to read later and Claire glanced at her watch and jumped to her feet.

'Whoa, look at the time. Less than five minutes to go. Sure you won't change your mind and come?'

'No, thanks. You can drool for both of us.'

Nathaniel walked centre stage and stared into the darkness. He didn't see the audience. He wasn't thinking about the critics.

He was King Richard II, the doomed king.

He opened his mouth to deliver his opening lines to John of Gaunt when a spotlight illuminated the front row of the audience.

Holding the crown in his hand, Nathaniel looked down and his eyes locked onto a familiar face. Familiar and yet unfamiliar. Twenty years had wrought changes, but not so many changes that the features were unrecognisable.

Shock froze time.

The features blurred.

And then the past rushed forward with terrifying speed and his concentration shattered like glass dropped onto concrete. The momentary lapse released a lethal cocktail of memories and they swirled around his head, delighted to be free after so many years incarcerated in the locked vault of his brain.

Shouts and terror. Stop it, stop it! And blood. Blood everywhere. Do something…

He felt helpless. Utterly helpless.

His heart pounding, Nathaniel stared down at his hands clasping the crown. There was no blood. His hands were clean. But still he couldn't move, his brain frozen by the ghosts of his own inadequacy. The knowledge that he hadn't acted, hadn't done something, gnawed at him....

Guilt crawled over him like a poisonous insect and he wondered how it was possible to shiver and sweat at the same time.

Dimly aware of the ripple of speculation that slowly spread through the audience, Nathaniel fought with ruthless determination to close down that side of himself.

Richard, he thought desperately. *King Richard.*

He gripped the crown and tried to slip back into his character's skin. But it no longer fitted him. Control slid from him like a cloak.

Each time he opened his eyes he saw the same face looking at him from the front row reminding him that he wasn't King Richard II—he was Nathaniel Wolfe, an actor with a family background more dramatic than anything penned even by the Bard himself.

If Shakespeare had been alive, Nathaniel thought bitterly, he would have written the Wolfe family history as a tragedy in three acts.

No comedy. No happy endings. Just life at its darkest.

Desperate now, he tried to claw his way through that darkness back to the surface but he could feel himself sinking, drowning in the thick mud of his past.

Why choose this moment to come back? Why now, when they'd all rebuilt their lives?

Anger ripped through him, hot and sharp.

He had to warn Annabelle. That, at least, he could do. He had to contact her right now.

The ripple of speculation grew to a restless buzz from the audience. People who had assumed he was pausing for maximum effect, suddenly realised that something was terribly wrong. Silence turned to murmur and murmur to conversation.

Bracing his shoulders like a fighter poised for impact, Nathaniel tried one more time to deliver his opening lines but he couldn't even remember them. Sucked back in time, the layer he put between himself and the world simply melted away.

Stripped of his camouflage, he was forced into the skin of the one character he'd avoided playing all his life.

Nathaniel Wolfe.

Last time, he'd let her down. This time, he wouldn't.

'Ladies and gentleman…' His voice, cold and devoid of emotion, carried to the back of the auditorium. He made a point of not looking at the man in the front row. It took all his self-control not to stride into the audience, grab him by the throat and knock him out cold. 'Tonight's performance is cancelled. Please see the box office for a refund.'

Having finished her preparation for the interview, Katie rolled her aching shoulders and left the wardrobe department. Backstage, the theatre was eerily quiet. Everyone was watching Nathaniel Wolfe.

She stood for a moment, breathing in the smells and the atmosphere. History was embedded deep in the fabric of the building. How many famous actors and actresses had trodden the boards of this theatre?

For a moment she was a child again, six years old and playing dress-up with her sister, Paula.

You can't be the princess, Katie, you're too fat and your hair is curly. I'm the prettiest so I'll be the princess. You can dress me.

What had started as duty fast became a passion. When Paula had decided it wasn't cool to hang out with her dumpy little sister, Katie had continued to dress her friends. Every night after school they'd put on plays, and Katie had been the one who decided what they were going to wear. She'd loved experimenting with different combinations, loved the challenge of designing a costume that conveyed the essence of each character. A princess with a sword. A fairy in breeches and boots. She'd listened to her friends discussing roles and knew instinctively which costume they needed to fully express the part. She'd dressed her friends, she'd dressed dolls, she'd dressed her mother…

The only person she never dressed again was Paula, whose modelling dreams had taken her far away from her humble roots.

But Katie had continued to dream.

A loud crash from the wings brought her back to the present.

Katie turned her head and listened. What began as a purposeful masculine stride, suddenly increased to a run.

Frowning, she stood her ground, ready to point out to whoever it was that the noise could probably be heard all the way across London's West End.

Who could possibly be running? An inexperienced stagehand, presumably. Or possibly one of the hangers-on who had been lingering backstage in the hope of catching a glimpse of Nathaniel Wolfe's virile, muscular frame and flawless features.

Realising that the footsteps were coming straight towards her, Katie hurriedly stepped out of the way but she was too late. A powerful male body slammed into her and sent her flying. There was no time to gasp or cry out. Falling backwards, she braced herself to hit the ground but strong hands suddenly grabbed her and hauled her upright, holding on until she was steady.

Trapped against hard, packed muscle, something melted inside her. It was an elemental reaction that transcended common sense and the sheer power of it shocked her.

Sharp bones, black hair and eyes that could make a woman forget her own name.

'Er, Mr Wolfe, I didn't expect to see you here. I mean, obviously you're performing here so I did expect to see you, but not exactly right here at this precise moment and especially not running backstage.' *Oh, shut up, Katie.* 'Is something wrong? Well, I can see something is wrong,' she blurted out, 'otherwise you wouldn't be thundering backstage like a herd of elephants, but—'

'He's here....' His hands gripped her shoulders so tightly that Katie winced.

'Er, who?' She stared up at him stupidly, her heart hammering against her chest and her mouth dry as dust. Up close it was impossible not to stare. He was shockingly sexy, every line of his perfect features accentuating his masculinity. She tried desperately to form a lucid sentence but her brain felt as if it had been anaesthetised. 'Mr Wolfe?'

'Why now?' Those blue eyes were two glittering slits of fierce anger. *'Why?'* He released her and punched his fist hard into a piece of abandoned scenery, splintering the wood. Breathing heavily, he pressed his fingers to his forehead, barely coherent. 'I can't—I don't—I have to warn Annabelle....'

Who was Annabelle?

'Right, well, I can see you're upset....' Katie took a wary step backwards, watching him as he drew his phone out of his pocket and keyed in a number. His knuckles were grazed and raw, but he didn't appear to have noticed. In that single moment, she understood why Nathaniel Wolfe excelled at playing deeply troubled heroes—underneath that perfect physique and breathtakingly handsome face he was a man every bit as troubled as the characters he portrayed. And that was part of the attraction, of course. There was a side of him that was untamed and dangerous. Registering the hard set of his jaw and the grim line of his mouth, she thought about the Special Forces soldier he'd played in his recent action thriller, *Alpha Man.*

He was the hunter.

And right now he wasn't acting. She *knew* he wasn't acting. And there was no point in her trying to persuade him back onstage. He was a man who followed no one's orders but his own.

Out of her depth, Katie glanced around, desperately hoping someone else would arrive and take over. Where were the stage managers?

He held the phone to his ear, his movements restless and edgy. Apart from onstage, acting, she'd only ever seen him supercool. He was occasionally sarcastic, frequently bored, but never out of control.

Right now, he looked out of control. The force field of cynicism that surrounded him had been replaced by something close to desperation.

'Is there an exit that the press don't know about?'

'Exit?' Katie tried to breathe but there was something about the intensity of his gaze that made it impossible to do anything except stare. This was closer than she'd ever been to him before and he was spectacular.

'If Carrie finds out, this whole thing is going to blow up—Answer the phone, damn it….' Clearly no one did and he left a short, cryptic message before pocketing the phone again. Then he grabbed Katie by the arm, his tone raw and desperate. 'You have to get me out of here. Fast.'

Still absorbing the fact that he obviously had two women on the go at the same time, Katie looked at him sternly and then froze because she saw desperation in his eyes. And knew she'd made a fundamental mistake in her assessment of him.

He wasn't the hunter.

He was the hunted.

Someone—or something—was chasing him.

'There's a fire escape in the wardrobe department. It leads into one of the side streets.' Without pausing to question her actions, she grabbed his hand and dragged him back into the wardrobe department, locking the door behind them.

'That will hold them for a few minutes. The fire escape is over there. Good luck.'

'I can't do this without help!' He yanked her up close. 'Where do you live? Is it far?'

The strength left her knees. 'You have to be kidding. I mean, you have a suite at The Dorchester and—'

'—and that is the first place they'll look. The press have been camped outside since my plane landed.'

Katie tried to imagine Nathaniel Wolfe in her cramped bedsit and her face burned. 'My place is really tiny. Honestly, I don't think—'

'Please.' He cupped her face in his hands so that she had no choice but to look at him again. Eye to eye, she was dazzled. Tumbling into that intense blue gaze, she forgot where she was. She forgot *who* she was. Dimly she remembered him asking her something but her eyes were locked with his and—

'Katie?'

In the grip of a sexual excitement she'd never experienced before, she swayed towards him. 'Mmm?'

'Katie!' He snapped his fingers in front of her face and broke the spell.

Shaking her head to clear the buzzing in her brain, Katie felt as though she was coming out of a trance.

'Y-you know my name.'

'I make a point of knowing the name of every woman who has ever taken my inside leg measurement.' Beneath the sardonic lift of his brows his eyes glinted. 'Get us out of here, angel. I don't want to be tonight's meal for the paparazzi.'

Always a sucker for anyone in trouble and totally bowled over by the fact he actually knew her name, Katie ignored the inner voice that was telling her it was a big mistake. 'All right, but my place is going to be a shock after The Dorchester. Don't say I didn't warn you.' She grabbed her jacket and two helmets and thrust one of them towards him. 'Take this.'

He stared at it blankly. 'What for?'

'If we're escaping, then we need an escape vehicle. I have one outside. It's nippy and great for getting through London traffic. Put the helmet on—it will cover your face. Not that your face isn't incredible to look at but—' Flustered, she pushed the helmet into his hands. 'This will be a lot easier.'

The voices were outside now and someone rattled the door.

Katie took matters into her own hands. She reached up and jammed the helmet onto his head. 'The fire escape will be icy. Watch your footing. I feel really stupid saying that to you—the guy who does most of his own stunts. I'm sure an icy fire escape isn't going to present you with a challenge.'

He had his phone in his hand again. 'I just need to make one more call….'

'You can make it when you get to my place.' Katie didn't point out that if he stuck to one woman at a time, then he wouldn't be in this desperate situation. Telling herself that his complicated love life was none of her business, she tugged at his arm. 'If you don't want to get up close and personal with a hundred camera lenses, then we need to get out of here now!'

CHAPTER TWO

THE sound of their feet echoed on the metal steps of the fire escape and Katie jumped the last few and landed in the alleyway next to her Vespa.

As the cold February air nipped through their clothing, Nathaniel stared at the scooter, one eyebrow raised in naked disbelief. '*That's* your idea of an escape vehicle?'

'It may not be a Ferrari, but—'

'It definitely isn't a Ferrari.'

'It's faster than it looks. And it has the added advantage that you wouldn't be seen dead on one, which means that no one will be expecting to see you on it.' As she swung her leg over the bike and fired up the engine, a pack of paparazzi came screaming round the corner like crazed animals.

Flashes exploded and Katie shrank. 'I don't want them to take my picture—I hate having my picture taken.'

Nathaniel vaulted onto the bike behind her, hooked his arm round her waist and pulled himself close. 'Move. That's if this thing is capable of moving.'

His hard body pressed against hers and awareness speared her from throat to pelvis. The raw burn of it shocked her. More powerful, more intense than anything she'd experienced before. Mortified to realise that he had his hand planted firmly on her stomach, Katie sucked it in and vowed that from now on she was going to do at least a hundred sit-ups a day.

Impatient, Nathaniel closed his hands over hers. 'Go!' Taking control, he twisted the throttle and the Vespa sprang forward with a force that threw Katie back against his chest. Caged by his strong arms and crushed against hard male muscle, some of the fear left her. Her helmet bumped against his shoulder and in that instant she thought about all the women in the world who would have given their life savings to swap places with her.

Surreal, she thought. *Nathaniel Wolfe on the back of her Vespa.*

And then suddenly she had a whole new reason to be afraid because he wasn't slowing down. Instead he was squeezing every last atom of speed from the bike. The wind blew in her face, the ends of her hair lifted.

'Slow down!' She hadn't known her tame, trusty little Vespa was capable of such speeds. Too late she remembered that Nathaniel Wolfe raced motorbikes as a hobby and that several directors refused to work with him because he was wild and a risk taker.

The bad, bad boy of Hollywood.

Fearless and bold he pushed her bike to its limits and Katie gave a whimper of panic. She didn't particularly like journalists, but she had no wish to kill anyone.

'Something wrong?' His laughing voice was close to her ear and she choked out one word.

'Speeding—'

'I'm doing my best, sweetheart, but next time do us both a favour and buy the fuel-injected version. This one sucks.'

They shot towards the crowd of journalists and Katie tried to scream but no sound emerged. Terrified, she tried to slacken back on the throttle but hard, strong fingers tightened on hers, controlling what she did, forcing her to maintain maximum speed.

'Relax.' His voice was molten seduction in her ear. 'They'll move.'

'And if they don't?'

'Then there'll be a few less journalists following me. Haven't you ever played chicken?'

'I'm vegetarian!' Katie squeezed her eyes tightly shut, coming to terms with the fact she was going to be the first person to get a speeding ticket on a Vespa. All she could hope was that she wouldn't earn herself a manslaughter charge to go with it.

Braced for impact, she thought to herself that the rumours about his physical strength hadn't been exaggerated. His hands were locked on hers in a death grip and the muscles of his shoulders were a solid wall behind her.

'Hang on,' he growled in her ear, and Katie opened her eyes to discover that they were now close enough to the photographers to see the whites of their eyes. At the last minute the crowd scattered and the bike shot through the sudden gap and emerged onto the main road. There was a shriek of tyres as people swerved to avoid them, a cacophony of taxi horns and several warning shouts, and Katie was glad his hands were over hers because her palms were slippery with sweat and she knew that if he weren't controlling the bike, then she would probably have just slid in a heap to the pavement.

She heard him laugh and decided right there and then that Nathaniel Wolfe had a sick sense of humour.

Outside the theatre there was a crowd of people, mostly women, many holding banners saying *I Love Nathaniel Wolfe.* They'd queued for hours in the hope of catching a glimpse of the Hollywood megastar as he left the theatre. They didn't seem to care that he was notorious for not signing autographs. All they wanted was to catch a glimpse of those famous eyes.

If they recognised him…

'Which way?' The voice next to her ear was firm and decisive and now it was her turn to take the lead because she knew these streets well. Soon she was weaving through the London traffic, putting as much distance as possible between her and the journalists. She turned off the main road and took an elaborate detour, choosing back roads and side streets.

As her heart gradually slowed and her panic eased, the enormity of what she'd done suddenly hit her.

It took twenty minutes to be sure that no one had followed her and another ten to double back across the river towards south London and her flat. And all the time she was aware of the heat of Nathaniel's body pressed against hers and his arm clamped around her waist.

He should have been cold, she thought, wearing only the leather jacket and black T-shirt that was the costume she'd selected for his contemporary portrayal of King Richard, but wherever their bodies touched, she felt warmth. Or maybe the warmth was hers. A fiery glow burned her skin through her clothing.

You're as susceptible as every other woman, Katie.

Pushing aside that unsettling thought, Katie swerved into an alleyway adjoining a block of flats.

'This is where I live.'

He swung his leg off the bike and unfastened the helmet.

'Don't take it off,' Katie said quickly. 'Someone might recognise you. Let's get inside first. Walk as if you're ordinary, not as if you're a movie star or a Special Forces soldier on a mission. You need to melt into the background.'

'I'm six foot two. Melting into the background isn't easy.'

Katie rolled her eyes as she slid off the bike, her legs as floppy as string. 'You drove like a maniac. I thought you were going to kill us both.' She locked her scooter. 'I'm on the second floor. Don't look at anyone.'

'I'm wearing the helmet.'

'But you can still see your eyes.' And those fierce blue eyes were known the world over. Slightly slanting and fringed by thick, dark lashes that simply intensified that hypnotic gaze, his eyes were designed for sin and seduction.

Katie tried not to look at him. It was easier to concentrate if she didn't look. 'Just…try and be invisible.' Their footsteps echoed around the stairwell and a door opened a slit as they passed.

'Is that you, Katie dear?'

Katie gestured to Nathaniel to stay back. 'It's me, Vera. Everything all right?'

'You're home already?' The door opened a little wider and the old lady peered through her glasses, 'And with a nice young man. That was quick. I suppose that's why it's called speed dating.'

'Vera—'

'I said to Maggie in 22A, if those guys have any sense they're going to all be taking our Katie's number.'

'Vera, I haven't—'

'And you brought him straight back home. No messing around. Good for you. I envy you modern girls. In my day we had to sit through long boring dates and we didn't even get sex at the end of it.' Vera leaned forward and squinted at Nathaniel. 'You look like a man who can handle himself. And you have good shoulders. I like a man with good shoulders.'

Melting with embarrassment and terrified that the old lady would recognise Nathaniel, Katie leaned forward and gave her neighbour a hug. 'Go back inside now. It's freezing tonight and you're letting all the heat out. I'll come and have a cup of tea with you soon.'

Vera was gazing at Nathaniel. 'You look a bit like that lovely young man everyone is raving about—that movie star. You could get a job as his body double or one of those lookalikes. We had a Tom Cruise lookalike at the Day Centre a few months ago but he was very disappointing. The eyes were all wrong.'

'Vera, we have to go….' Katie backed away.

'Well, of course you do.' Vera gave a knowing wink. 'You have things to do. Speed dating. Just remember, not everything has to be done fast.' She closed the door and Katie pulled her keys out of her pocket, so embarrassed she didn't know where to look.

Flicking on the light, her embarrassment increased when she saw the state of the place. Pictures from her sketchbook were spread all over the floor from her late-night working session and dirty bowls and plates were still stacked in the sink waiting to be washed.

'Sorry about the mess.' Still not looking at him she closed the door behind them. 'I did the early shift at the coffee shop yesterday and then I was working on a costume plot for a new production of *The Taming of the Shrew.* I didn't have time to clear up.'

'A shift at the coffee shop?'

'I start at six. Mostly serving double-shot cappuccinos to tired commuters. Look, just give me a minute and I'll clear the place up.'

Nathaniel dragged off the helmet and picked up the drawing closest to him. 'Don't you work on computer?'

'Yes, but I prefer to draw when I can, especially in the early stages of design. It's very important to understand what the costume says about the character.'

'This dress says "I like hot sex."' He studied the drawing. 'If that's for Katherine I'd say Petruchio is in for a good night. So…you were supposed to be speed dating tonight?'

Katie snatched the drawing out of his hand. 'I was just going to keep a friend company.' She changed the subject quickly. 'Do you think anyone followed us?'

'I think you managed to lose them. You could give a few lessons to my security team.' He was cool and relaxed, almost bored, as if the entire escape plan had been engineered solely for her entertainment. There was no sign of the desperation he'd shown at the theatre. Instead he strolled around her tiny living room, examining photographs, picking up a book she'd left lying face down, glancing at a stack of magazines.

Magazines.

Katie froze in horror, but it was too late. He'd already picked up the one from the top of the pile. The one with the photograph of him naked from the waist up as Alpha Man.

'Why do you have pictures of me?'

Because she was human. Because she was a woman…

'I used them for costume design.' She fished around for a plausible reason. 'I had to study your features—decide which styles and colours would look best for the part of King Richard.' *At least she hadn't stuck the pictures to her wall.*

He put the magazine down and picked up another of her drawings. 'You're good.'

Relieved that he hadn't gone through the rest of the magazines and discovered just how many photos of him she'd collected, Katie stood rigid and self-conscious as Nathaniel looked slowly round her small cramped one-bed apartment.

'Interesting choice of decor.' He lifted one of the red silk cushions piled on her sofa. 'What is this place—the harem? Are you auditioning for a part as the sheikh's concubine or something?'

Katie felt herself turn the same shade as the cushion. She so rarely brought anyone back home that it hadn't occurred to her to think how it might look through someone else's eyes. 'I don't think I'm sheikh's concubine material.' *She didn't have enough experience to be anyone's concubine.* 'The place was kind of tired and depressing when I moved in. I got a bit carried away trying to make it homely.' She'd used her creative flair to make the cramped space welcoming. To conceal the damp patches she'd tacked fabric to the wall. The threadbare carpet was now covered by a large rug in deep shades of exotic red. Lamps provided subtle lighting and drew the eye away from the watermark on the ceiling. The single sofa had been left there by the previous occupants and she'd simply covered it with a bright throw and piles of jewel-coloured cushions that she'd made herself from scraps of fabric.

Imagining what he must be thinking, Katie blushed. 'It

doesn't look like much, but actually the area isn't too bad as long as you stay indoors after midnight. And it's cheap—I'm paying off some debts at the moment. My dad died last year, which was devastating enough, and I only discovered after he died that he'd had a gambling problem for most of his life....' A lump lodged in her throat. 'Anyway, he'd borrowed money against the house and if I miss a payment the house gets repossessed and my mum loses her home...so I'm working pretty hard.'

He looked slightly stunned. 'Do you always tell your life story to strangers?'

'If they stand still long enough to hear it,' Katie said lamely. 'Sorry. I don't mean to bore you. I'm just trying to explain why there hasn't been a lot of housekeeping going on around here.'

His gaze lingered on the unwashed cereal bowl in the sink. 'Breakfast?'

'Last night's dinner.' Katie replied without thinking. 'If I'm home late I can't always be bothered to cook so I just have cereal. Or toast. You know what it's like when you're on your own....' Remembering who she was talking to, she gave an awkward shrug. 'Actually, you probably don't. If *you're* on your own you probably go to a five-star restaurant....' Digging herself deeper and deeper into a hole, she felt herself turn redder and redder. 'Except that a guy like you is probably never on his own...and anyway, no one in Hollywood ever eats carbs, I know that, so cereal and toast would be—'

'Do you ever stop talking?' He was watching her with those sexy slanting eyes that made grown women lose their grip on reality. And his mouth—*oh, God, his mouth...*

Katie clamped her own mouth shut. This was her opportunity to intrigue him with scintillating conversation. At the very least she ought to be talking about something intelligent like films, global warming or space exploration. Instead she was talking about breakfast cereal.

'Sorry. I'm just not used to having a movie star in my living room. It feels—'

'How does it feel?' The way he was looking at her turned her insides to liquid. His eyes slid to her mouth and Katie felt the blood pound through her veins. Being the focus of his attention was the most heady, exciting thing that had ever happened to her. He was looking at her as if, as if—

Oh, God, Nathaniel Wolfe was going to kiss her.

Why, oh, why, hadn't she stuck to her diet?

Wound tight with sexual awareness, she swayed towards him. She saw him lower his head towards hers and then he gave a sharp frown and turned away abruptly, walking to the far side of the room.

Katie stood like an idiot, completely thrown off balance. What had she expected? Nathaniel Wolfe was a superstar. What on earth had made her think he'd want to kiss someone like her? Clearly she was delusional.

Delusional and untidy.

Absorbing the state of her flat in horror, she vowed that from now on she was going to be more organised in her home life. No more getting lost in work and losing track of the time. No more spreading her drawings over the floor. Taking advantage of the fact he had his back to her, she dropped stealthily to her knees and started scooping up papers.

And then he turned. Their eyes met and held.

The papers slipped from her hands. 'I told you you'd be better off at The Dorchester. You probably think I'm a mess, but I don't have a desk and I find it easier to spread out so that I can see the character progression.' Realising that he was just staring at her blankly, she sat back on her heels. 'You look awful,' she muttered. 'Are you sure you don't want to talk about it? You seemed pretty upset in the theatre. If something is bothering you it's better to let it spill out, instead of bottling it up.'

Those famous blue eyes were blank of expression. 'Nothing is bothering me.'

Liar. Katie remembered the way he'd looked in the theatre. 'You don't have to pretend with me. When Dad died last year I would have gone under if it hadn't been for my friends.' She gathered up the papers again and stood. 'Do you want my humble opinion on the situation?'

'You have an opinion on my situation?'

'I can only give you the female point of view.' Katie hugged the drawings to her chest. 'You mentioned Annabelle and Carrie, so I assume you're seeing two women at the same time…' She paused, waiting for him to contradict her but he simply stared at her so she stumbled on. 'That's only ever going to end badly, even if you're a movie star, but obviously that's up to you, and frankly my love life is such a disaster I wouldn't dream of passing judgement on anyone else's, but I *would* say that I think it's a seriously bad move to get involved with a married woman.'

A tiny muscle flickered at the corner of his mouth. 'What makes you think I'm involved with a married woman?'

'The way you rushed off the stage. You looked as though you'd seen Hamlet's ghost and you said something like—' Katie wrinkled her nose as she tried to remember. "He's here." Yes, that's right, you said, "He's here." Then you were muttering about needing to warn Annabelle and something about Carrie not finding out, so I assumed that the "he" you referred to must be a jealous husband—and then you punched a hole in a piece of scenery.' She glanced at his hand. 'Which reminds me, I'd better get you some ice for that before it swells up.' Putting down the drawings, she walked over to the fridge and pulled out a small packet of frozen peas.

'You have an overactive imagination,' he said harshly. 'When I said, "He's here," I was referring to a theatre critic from one of the newspapers—really nasty guy. I suddenly realised that I wasn't ready to play the part. Filming on my last project overran and that cut into the rehearsal schedule. We just weren't ready. I stood there and it felt wrong.'

It didn't make sense to Katie. 'I saw you in rehearsal. You were incredible. Are you trying to say you had an attack of stage fright?'

'More an attack of artistic integrity. I'm a perfectionist. If it isn't going to be perfect, I won't do it.' His eyes were a deep, mesmerising blue and they drew her in, demanding her trust. It was like being hypnotised.

Katie felt her doubts fade.

If he said it was all about the performance, then maybe it was. Actors, singers—all artists were the same, weren't they? Focused on themselves and their craft.

And then she remembered that this man had won awards for his acting skills.

And he was acting now.

A mesmerising, compelling gaze didn't mean he was telling the truth. It meant that he wanted her to believe him. *Not* the same thing.

Her first impression had been correct. His reaction at the theatre was genuine. Under the surface, the tension was still there. And then there had been that phone call—the phone call she'd tried not to listen to—sparse on information but loaded with tension and urgency.

He's back.

Why would he say that about a theatre critic? And which one of his many women had he been talking to? His love life was obviously a complete mess.

Katie pressed the icy bag of peas to his hand. 'That looks really painful. Do you think you've broken something?'

'It's nothing.' He snapped out the words. 'What else did you overhear?'

'I don't know. Don't stress out about it. It doesn't matter.'

'Trust me, it matters.'

'Why?'

'Because I've just discovered you can talk for England.'

'That doesn't mean I'm going to say anything about you. It isn't as if I even know Annabelle or Carrie so it isn't going to be awkward. The only thing I know is that they're going to be pretty upset when they find out about each other but I daresay they'll punish you in whatever way they see fit. The other day I read about this woman in Chicago who found out her husband was seeing someone else, and she—'

'Do you *ever* stop talking?'

Skewered by his lethal tone, Katie froze. 'I talk when I'm nervous and you're making me really nervous.'

'*How* am I making you nervous?'

'Just by being here!' Her voice rose. 'It's pretty weird having a movie star in my living room. I keep waiting for someone to shout, "Action!"'

His eyes grew slumberous. 'You're looking for action?'

Her body warmed and the room suddenly felt dangerously claustrophobic. 'I just mean this whole thing feels surreal. You, here. I warned you it wasn't The Dorchester.'

'If I wanted The Dorchester, that's where I'd be.'

Her living room seemed to have shrunk to half its size. She was aware of every movement he made—of every glance and every shift in his facial expression. 'Look—' she backed away '—I know you're desperate to phone your many women, so I'll just leave you to get on with it.'

'Thanks.' There was a heavy note of sarcasm to his voice that she didn't understand and she decided just to make herself scarce. There was a restlessness about him that was making her uneasy.

'I'll be—' she waved a hand vaguely '—in the bedroom if you need me.' *Oh, for crying out loud, Katie, think before you speak.*

A sardonic gleam lit those blue eyes. 'In the bedroom—ready for action?'

Was he actually flirting with her?

No, of course he wasn't. She was having delusions again. Not looking at him, Katie shot into the bedroom and closed the door.

The powerful surge of lust astonished him.

What the hell was he doing, flirting with a woman who had pictures of him in her home?

It was asking for trouble and he already had more than enough of that.

He'd been running on adrenalin since that moment he'd walked off the stage and now the tension was a white-hot ball inside him. His carefully constructed life was crashing down around him like a full-scale demolition programme. There were things he needed to do and people he needed to speak to.

So why did his hand burn to reach for the door handle rather than his phone?

Why was he gripped by an inexplicable urge to break down that damn door and lose himself in her gorgeous breasts and sweet smile?

It didn't help that she wanted him too. Experienced at dealing with women far more sophisticated than Katie, he'd read her easily—seen the exact moment her pupils dilated and sexual awareness had darkened those lovely eyes. He'd also seen how hard she was fighting that reaction.

Nathaniel gave a bitter smile.

He hoped she was having more success than he was. Right now, sex was the last thing he needed.

Hands thrust in his pockets, he stepped back from her bedroom door, disconcerted by the sheer strength of that craving.

He was no saint when it came to his relationships with women, but he knew better than to mess around with a woman who looked at him as if he had a first-class ticket to the end of the rainbow.

There were no rainbows in his life. Only thunderclouds. At the moment those thunderclouds were threatening a storm like no other.

Nathaniel checked his phone again, but there was no response from Annabelle. Had she even picked up the message? *Was she huddled in a heap somewhere, shivering with reaction?*

He felt the bite of guilt, as he always did when he thought of Annabelle, and something deeper, something uglier—something moulded deep inside himself.

Pushing the phone back into his pocket, he wondered why he was even bothering trying to contact her. It wasn't as if they were close. None of the Wolfe siblings did 'close.' The only common thread they shared was fierce independence. A reluctance to bond with anyone.

Nathaniel paced across the flat and glanced out of the window but the streets were empty apart from a loan woman slipping and sliding on the icy streets as she struggled against the icy wind.

There were no paparazzi. Miss Chatterbox-with-the-gorgeous-breasts had managed to lose them.

He stared blankly out of the window, and by the time the bedroom door opened again he had himself under control.

It was immediately obvious that she'd renewed her make-up and then scrubbed it off, afraid it would look as if she were trying too hard. Nathaniel gave a humourless laugh. She didn't need to try. Make-up or no make-up, her mouth was still the same full tempting curve that made a man want to dive straight in and sample the flavour. Even seeing her wild, curling hair tied back in an unflattering ponytail didn't kill the chemistry. All that chatter and unusual openness should have irritated him. Instead she was getting under his skin.

He wondered what she'd say if she knew how close he was to hauling her back into the bedroom. He wanted to lose himself. *He wanted distraction from the mess that was his life.*

'Are you—?' She cleared her throat, careful not to look at him. 'Are you going to answer that?'

Answer what?

Drowning in his private hell, Nathaniel realised that his phone was ringing and he hadn't even noticed.

It was his brother Sebastian and this time he took the call, conscious that Katie would be listening to every word of the conversation. 'Yes, he was there.…Rafael must have given him the ticket.… I've no idea. All we can do is manage the situation.' As he talked, Katie busied herself in the kitchen area, clattering away, trying not to listen. She was still wearing her skinny jeans and her bottom was a smooth curve straight from a bad boy's fantasy. Deep in that fantasy, Nathaniel realised he'd missed half of what his brother had said. 'Sorry?… No, that's way too risky. I'm going to leave the country. I'll be in touch and you have my private number.… The most important thing is that we protect her.'

What the hell was the matter with him? He should be concentrating on damage limitation, not working out ways to remove Katie from those jeans.

He pocketed the phone. 'Do you have any bourbon?'

Still with her back to him, she stacked a week's supply of breakfast bowls. 'Sorry, no.' Her slender shoulders were stiff and Nathaniel felt a flash of irritation.

'Look at me, will you?'

'The only way I can behave even remotely normally is if I don't look at you. Sorry if that seems rude, but that's just the way it is. I don't have bourbon but I do have water, or—' Still not looking at him, she tugged open the fridge. 'Milk?'

'I haven't drunk a glass of milk since I was three years old.'

'It's full of calcium and vitamin D. Good for your bones.'

'Alcohol is good for my stress levels. What's this?' He

picked up a bottle of red wine that was sitting on the side and read the label.

She glanced over her shoulder, the movement sending the ponytail swinging. 'You won't be interested in that. It could double as paint stripper.'

Nathaniel was tempted to confess that the way he felt right at that moment he would have considered the paint stripper. 'It can't be that bad.' Without waiting to be asked, he reached past her and grabbed two glasses from the cupboard. The scent of her wound itself around his senses and he tried to block his reaction.

She closed the fridge and moved away carefully. 'Don't pour one for me.'

Wondering how sexual tension could still throb when two people weren't looking at each other, Nathaniel ignored her and poured two glasses. 'Drink. We both need it.' He took a large mouthful and winced as his palate was assaulted by flavours not normally associated with wine. 'On second thoughts, maybe we don't need it.'

'I've changed my mind. I think I do.' Visibly flustered, she picked up her glass and drank.

'Clearly you don't have a very discerning palate.'

'I can't afford a discerning palate, Mr Wolfe.'

'What's it going to take to get you to look at me?'

Still holding the glass, she stared at a point in the centre of his chest. 'I just—I'm finding it really hard to behave normally with you. Sorry, but…aren't you finding this at all odd?'

'What's odd about it?'

'Well, I'm me.' With a rueful smile, she glanced down at herself. 'Jeans with a hole, tiny flat, modest job. And you're—well, you know who you are. Let's just say I feel as though I should buy a ticket before I'm allowed to look at you. I associate you with movies. I keep waiting for some bad guy to leap out from behind you with a gun.'

'Talking of guys leaping out from behind me, is some

jealous lover built like a sumo wrestler likely to turn up later and want to beat me to a pulp? Presumably not, as you're speed dating.'

'I live alone. Number of jealous lovers—zero. I'm going through a lean patch. Well, not lean as in *lean*, obviously.' The words spilled out, uncensored. 'Lean as in not much action. And not action as in—'

'So you're single.' Why was he asking? *Why the hell was he doing this to himself?*

'Completely single. Not that I mind being single,' she added hastily, clearly worried he might think she was dropping hints. 'Being single is good. I can do anything I like without having to check with anyone. I can be spontaneous. I can eat cereal for supper and wash up the breakfast things when I'm ready and until today no one ever knew or cared, although—' she gave a tiny smile '—obviously from now on I'll be tidier just in case a Hollywood star happens to drop by. And, being single, if I want to go and—and—well, whatever I want to go and do, I do it. Sorry. Talking too much again…' Her voice faded and she shrugged awkwardly. 'The short answer to your question is yes, I live alone. And now I've said that I'm realising that actually you're a complete stranger and I've invited you into my home. And that is why this is weird. I feel I know you because I've spent so long staring at you in movies. I've seen you naked, but I don't know you at all.'

'You've seen me naked?' The nerves on the back of his neck prickled. This wasn't the way he'd intended the conversation to go. He should be on the phone, sorting out his monumental personal crisis, not flirting with a girl who had *romantic* stamped all over her.

'You did that indie film.' She stared down into her glass. 'I think I saw it once—or maybe twice…' The colour of her cheeks told him she'd watched it at least a hundred times. 'The bit where you carried the daughter down to the beach was a bit of a cult scene when I was at university.'

Nathaniel struggled valiantly not to return the favour and imagine her naked. It didn't help that they were having the conversation surrounded by red silk cushions and a deep, inviting sofa. Gritting his teeth, he blanked out a sudden image of him taking her, there and then, on that sofa. 'I thought you studied costume design. Talk to me about what you do.' Talk about something. *Anything.* Anything, but sex.

'The naked body can be a costume—' she sounded breathless '—if it fits the role. All I'm saying is that it's weird to have seen you naked and yet actually not know you at all. You could be—well, I just don't know you, that's all.'

He bit back the suggestion that they get to know each other better. His life didn't have room for any more complications. It was already a mess and looking to get worse.

'You've worked with me for the past month so I'm not a stranger and I can assure you I don't have any nasty habits,' he drawled softly. 'Don't make the mistake of mixing me up with the parts I play. That's not who I am. Just for the record, the only time I'd rip your clothes off is if you were ripping mine off too.' *And right now that sounded like a damn good idea.*

'Honestly, I'm not thinking for one moment that you're going to rip my clothes off. I may be dreamy but I'm not delusional. I can distinguish between reality and fantasy, although—' she kept it light '—there were definitely moments on my scooter when you seemed to think you were Alpha Man. Do people often do that? Mix you up with the parts you play? Mix fantasy with reality?'

'All the time. The worst one was when I played a psychopathic doctor in *Heartsink*. For months people were coming up to me and asking me to diagnose their rashes.' They were no longer talking about sex, so why was his body still throbbing? And why couldn't he stop looking at her? 'I haven't thanked you for what you did tonight.'

'You're welcome.'

He was used to people behaving oddly around him—sometimes they were giggly, sometimes they were plain hysterical—but Katie was the first woman he'd met who was determined not to look at him. Exasperation flickered through him. 'It's really hard having a conversation with the top of your head.'

Finally she looked at him. Their eyes met and the explosion of awareness was mutual and instantaneous. 'Are you feeling a bit better?'

'Better?'

'At the theatre you were incredibly stressed.'

'Now you *are* delusional.' He changed the subject smoothly. 'Or maybe it's the wine. How many glasses do you need to drink before you do the dance of the seven veils?'

Her laugh was nervous. 'Your harem already seems a little crowded.'

'It's not crowded. Let me know any time you want me to play sheikh to your concubine. I could throw you over my shoulder and ravish you on that pile of silk cushions.' *And he was sorely tempted.*

Who cared if she had pictures of him? He was more than willing to give her the real thing.

'The sofa is really uncomfortable. Hence the cushions.' Her cheeks were the same shade of scarlet as those cushions.

'In that case I'll make sure I'm the one on top.' Without thinking, Nathaniel lifted his hand and stroked her face thoughtfully. 'You're very pretty. That's why the Duchess of Gloucester has been so irritable for the past month. She hates working with people who remind her she's ageing.' His hand lingered and he saw her lips part as she snatched in a shallow breath.

It would have been so easy to kiss her....

So easy...

'So—' she backed away from him, snapping the tension '—er, what are your plans tonight?'

He found her tendency to speak without thinking surprisingly endearing. In his world, no one spoke without thinking. 'I need somewhere to stay.'

'Oh—'

'That was your cue to invite me.'

'You want to stay *here*?' Her voice was a squeak. 'Are you mad? You could be in the penthouse suite at The Dorchester ordering room service and wallowing in luxury.'

Or he could be lying on her decadent sofa, listening to the rain and wondering whether she slept naked or not. 'Privacy is luxury. Can I sleep on your sofa?'

Her mouth opened and closed. 'You don't have any luggage. No pyjamas or anything.'

He managed to subdue the smile. 'I don't own pyjamas. So is that a yes?'

'I—well, if that's really what you want.' She looked faint, and despite the dark clouds rolling into his life he couldn't resist teasing her.

'And if I'm cold in the night?'

Their eyes met. He watched the dreams chase across her face just before she gave a little shake of her head.

'I'll go and fetch you some blankets. You won't be cold.'

CHAPTER THREE

HE WAS drowning.

The cold waters of the lake closed over his head, a murky coffin pulling him down to his death. As he opened his mouth to scream, the water poured into his lungs and the last thing he saw was the figure of a man as he walked away and left him to die.

Nathaniel woke drenched in sweat and shivering. Every bone in his body ached and his muscles screamed a protest at having been cramped in such an unforgiving position for a whole night. Despite the blankets, he was bitterly cold. His head ached from the after-effects of cheap wine and lack of sleep but he didn't care. He was just relieved to be awake. If sleep meant the nightmare, then he'd choose insomnia every time.

He ran his hand over his face, still gripped by images of the lake. The vision lurked at the back of his head, refusing to fade. It had been years since he'd returned to the place—years since he'd had the dream. It depressed him to know that it was still lurking in the corners of his brain, waiting to burst to life. All it had taken was Jacob's return.

Why the hell had he come back?

And why now?

Through the gap in the curtains Nathaniel caught a glimpse of a miserably wet February morning. The sky was a cheerless grey and he could hear rain sheeting against the window. He thought longingly of his enormous and extremely comfortable bed in his Californian home. He'd built a different life for himself and yet happiness was always just beyond the horizon. He'd thought doing live theatre would be a welcome change from the empty glass bubble that was Hollywood. He'd thought that in London he'd be safe from his past—he hadn't reckoned on the past watching him from the front row on opening night.

Nathaniel stared up at the ceiling, reliving the moment when he'd been stranded in the spotlight, staring trouble in the face while a flabbergasted audience watched in shocked fascination.

Pulling his phone out of his pocket, he found a text from Annabelle, sent in the cold dark hours of the night. Just two words.

I know.

Nathaniel stared at the message, wondering what state she'd been in when she'd sent it.

Chased by his own thoughts, plagued by that feeling of powerlessness, he sprang from the sofa and stood for a moment in the centre of the tiny living room, forcing himself to breathe. He'd never been in a room where the walls were so close together. He was trapped with only his thoughts for company.

And he hated his thoughts.

A shout came from outside and Nathan moved silently to the window and glanced through a gap in the curtains to the street below.

Journalists and photographers were gathered four-deep, lenses poised, a sense of excitement in the air.

They were calling his name.

Nathaniel leaned back against the wall, cursing fluently, wondering why he was surprised. It was part of his life, wasn't it? In no country in the world could he walk down the street unrecognised. And there was always someone willing to sell his whereabouts to a gossip magazine.

He glanced towards the closed bedroom door, his mouth tightening as he remembered how much she'd talked the night before.

'Nathaniel! Katie!'

Hearing her name shouted alongside his, Nathaniel felt a flash of anger and launched himself towards the door she'd closed between them the night before. Without bothering to knock, he strode into the room. 'Wake up, Sleeping Beauty. We've got crowd control issues.'

She came awake in an instant, her tousled dark curls spilling over her bare shoulders and her green eyes still dazed with sleep. 'What? Who?'

Beautiful, Nathaniel thought, momentarily distracted by the arresting sight of a sleepy female. For a moment he thought she slept naked and then he caught a glimpse of the tiny lace straps of a camisole through the soft tumbling hair.

'Thanks to your inability to keep a secret, we have company.' Gripped by a vicious attack of lust, Nathaniel turned away and banged his elbow sharply on the wall. Pain arced up his arm and through his shoulder. The place was so cramped he could hardly move. He eyed the narrow single bed in disbelief. 'How do you have sex in a bed that narrow?'

'What do you mean, crowd control issues?' She ignored his question. 'What are you talking about?'

'Photographers.' Three sketchbooks were stacked by her bed. Everywhere he looked there were sketches of glamorous dresses and yet he'd never seen her in anything other than jeans and boring tops. 'Our own little pack of journalists have hunted us down and now they're staking out the place, waiting to get a really revealing picture. You're looking particularly savoury this morning, wardrobe. If you stand in front of the window like that you might even make the front page.'

'Journalists?' His words finally penetrated and she shot upright, her eyes wide. 'Here? How did they find us?'

'Surprising, isn't it? Or perhaps it isn't so surprising given that you warned me you talk too much when you're nervous. They're also yelling your name,' he drawled, 'so don't waste your time pretending you don't know how they got here.'

'*My* name?' She froze and stared at him, her lips parted as she drew in uneven breaths. 'Oh, no—'

'Oh, *yes*.'

'I did *not* call the press.'

'Well, someone did, angel, because they're banging on the door as we speak.'

She flung the covers back and he had a glimpse of legs long enough to make a man lose his grip on reality. Dragging his eyes from slender perfection, he encountered pretty lacy underwear and then she was pulling on the same brown jumper and jeans she'd worn the day before. Sexy underwear—boring choice of clothes, Nathaniel thought absently. Strange.

'*Stop* looking at me.' With a flick of her hands, she freed her hair from her jumper. 'Give me some privacy.'

'Like you gave me privacy?' Ruthlessly shutting down his libido, Nathaniel folded his arms and watched her performance with grim-faced anger. 'I need to know what you told them.' The thought of what discovery might do to fragile Carrie sent a blast of cold anger through his system.

He'd promised he'd protect her and instead he'd exposed her.

'You think *I* called them?' She pushed her feet into brown pumps. *'Are you mad?'*

'Right now I'd describe my mood as moderately evil.'

'*You* were the one who grabbed *me*! You were the one who begged me to bring you here and let you stay the night—'

'I've never begged a woman in my life,' Nathaniel said coldly, 'and when I asked for your help at the theatre I was under the impression that you were a sweet, helpful young thing.' He tilted his head and gave a smile loaded with ironic self-mockery. 'But now we've cleared up that gross misconception, answer my question—who exactly did you phone and what *did* you tell them?'

'No one! Nothing!' Her voice rose and the horror in her eyes was replaced by anger. 'This is all your fault. You put me in this position.'

'The position of being able to make a mint from selling me out to the press?'

'I drove halfway round London last night to try and avoid the press. Why would I bother doing that if I was just going to call them anyway?'

'You tell me.'

'You think I brought you safely back here to my "lair" so that I could call the press, is that right? You think that's why I helped you?'

'If that isn't why you helped me, then tell me why you did.'

'Honestly? I don't know. Clearly I had a moment of extreme insanity.' Her voice was shrill. 'At the moment I wish I hadn't helped you because I certainly didn't need this in my life. I'm not the sort of person who wants to pose in front of a camera! And I don't know why you're so keen to believe the worst of me. Why would I sell you out?'

'People do it all the time, usually as they snap a picture of me on their phone.'

'I don't even have a camera on my phone! It switches on and off and that's about all it does.' Her hands in her hair, she sank down onto the edge of the bed. 'I don't want them printing my picture. I *hate* having my picture taken.'

Nathaniel drew in a breath. 'How much of my phone conversation did you hear? When you were in the bedroom, were you listening at the door?'

'Do you have any idea how offensive you are?' Her eyes were very green and very angry. 'I do *not* listen at doors. I am a very decent person and I have the utmost respect for the privacy of the individual.'

'You were in the bedroom for ages. What were you doing?'

Her cheeks reddened. 'I was staring in the mirror feeling about the size of a spec of dust because I had Alpha Man in my living room and I was looking like something that had been pulled through a hedge backwards.' She rubbed her hands over her knees in an agitated movement. 'You want to know what I was doing in the bedroom? I was wishing I was someone else—like a beautiful, long-legged actress-model-type, someone with visible hip bones who wouldn't have been phased to be entertaining Hollywood royalty.'

Distracted, Nathaniel looked at her in bemusement. 'Visible hip bones?'

'Yes. Skinny women always have visible hip bones. I've tried for *years* to get visible hip bones but frankly I like food too much to starve myself and it can't be natural to go round with your stomach rumbling the whole time, and normally I'm fine with the fact that I have hips and a bottom, but last night I let myself be intimidated by you and I *hate* myself for that because underneath that handsome face you're just an ego on legs who thinks that everything in the world is about him—'

'Katie—'

'I wasn't listening to your conversation, but in future if you're that worried, *don't* make calls when you have an audience, *don't* have an affair with two women at once and *don't* pull innocent bystanders into it.'

Trying to ignore the incessant throb in his head, Nathaniel pressed his fingers to the bridge of his nose, vowing never to drink cheap wine again. 'I am not having an affair with two women at once.' He spoke with lethal emphasis. 'Listen—'

'No, you listen! You want to know why I helped you last night? It was because you looked desperate. For once, you weren't all remote and sarcastic. You weren't *acting.*' Shivering, she rubbed her hands over her arms. 'And I hate the way the press hound you. They've been camped outside the theatre since the day you arrived. You can't even breathe without them watching and actually I don't think that's fair. That's why I helped you. And then I get you back here and suddenly you're acting as if nothing is wrong and I'm imagining everything and I'm starting to wonder if I've gone mad.' The words came tumbling out unrestricted and Nathaniel suppressed the urge to flatten her to her single bed and turn all that red-hot passion into something physical.

'If you didn't tip off the press, then who did?'

'How would I know? I haven't even spoken to any—' She broke off in midsentence and a look of horror crossed her face, quickly replaced by guilt. 'Oh, no…'

Nathaniel's mouth compressed. 'So you *did* call someone.'

'No.' Her eyes slid nervously to his. 'But someone called me.'

'And you couldn't help confiding. You're a girl, and girls just can't help gossiping to one another. It's that whole female bonding thing. Men share a beer. Girls share secrets.'

'No! I didn't share anything.' Her eyes were wide with dismay. 'My friend Claire rang when I was in the bedroom. We were supposed to be going speed dating together and she wanted to know where I was. Apparently the whole theatre was in a state of uproar because you'd vanished. She asked me if you were here but I denied it.'

He sighed. 'Not a born liar, are you? I need to give you acting lessons.'

'Claire would not have said anything,' she said loyally. 'No way.'

'Well, someone did.'

'Yes, but—' Katie broke off and frowned. 'The Duchess of Gloucester.'

'I beg your pardon?'

'Claire mentioned that the Duchess of Gloucester was revelling in the fact that you'd walked out. She was nearby when Claire phoned so it's possible she overheard. And it's not as if she likes you.' Rubbing her forehead, she gave a regretful groan. 'I'm so sorry. This *is* all my fault. I shouldn't have brought you back here. I was crazy to think we could keep it a secret.'

'No, it's mine.' *He should have known better.* If he'd been thinking, he wouldn't have involved anyone else. But he hadn't been thinking. He'd seen Jacob in the front row and reacted. 'As you say, I was the one who forced you to help me.'

'But I shouldn't have answered the phone. I should have been more convincing when she asked if I knew where you were. On the other hand, they probably would have guessed anyway.' Her eyes were bleak and tired. 'Last night, you and I were the only two people missing. The cast would have known that. And the press saw us together. It wouldn't have taken much for them to work out who I was and tracked us down to this address.'

Forced to concede that such a scenario was not only possible but probable, Nathaniel tried to be practical. 'They're here. We have to deal with it. They're camped outside the front of the flat and they know you spent the night with me.'

'*What?* I did *not* spend the night with you.'

'Yes, you did.'

'Well, yes, but not in *that way.* They're not going to think that for one minute. I mean, there's you, a global sex object, and then there's me—I'm not a global anything.' Self-conscious, she pushed her hair out of her eyes. 'No one in their right mind is going to think you spent the night with me so don't worry about that.'

'You're incredibly sexy.'

Her eyes widened with shock and her lips parted. 'You—you think *I'm* sexy?'

'Last night both of us were struggling to keep our hands off each other.'

'*No!* I mean, I— You didn't—' Her cheeks were scarlet. 'You're Nathaniel Wolfe.'

'What does that have to do with sexual chemistry?'

'Well, because—because…' She gave a hysterical, disbelieving laugh. 'I've seen pictures of the women you date and they're very depressing to look at.'

'Equally depressing to be with. Perhaps it's because they don't eat breakfast,' Nathaniel drawled mockingly. 'And you're definitely underestimating your own charms. The press are going to take one look at you and assume we've been swinging from the chandeliers all night.' Looking at her lush mouth he wished he hadn't settled for the lumpy sofa. 'They're going to want to hear your story.'

And she was such a talker, she'd tell it. And that would be disastrous.

She didn't know much, but she knew enough to bring his nightmare to life. The fact that she'd drawn all the wrong conclusions was no consolation to someone who understood the unstoppable force of the media.

He thought about the number of years he'd kept his secret. *He thought about the possible consequences of discovery.*

There was no way he could leave Katie here alone and at their mercy. No way.

Katie tiptoed over to the window. 'Stop worrying. I don't have a story. *Movie Star Sleeps on Holey Sofa.* I can't see that headline grabbing anyone by the throat.'

'*Don't* look out of the window.'

Ignoring him, she peeped through the curtains. 'Holy crap.' Flattening herself against the wall she looked at him in horror. 'There are *millions* of them. Are you really that interesting?'

'Apparently.'

'There are really important things going on in the world

and half the world's press is outside on the pavement.' Still plastered to the wall, she seemed afraid to move. 'I wish I'd never helped you. They're going to take my photograph and everyone will make comparisons.'

'Comparisons with whom?'

She stared at him, her breathing rapid. 'Nothing…this is a mess…'

'For once, we agree.' Nathaniel contemplated that truth with grim resignation. 'You're the female equivalent of an unexploded bomb. If I leave you here you could go off at any moment.'

Her spine was stiff. 'If you're implying that I'd tell them anything, then you're wrong.'

'I thought we'd established that you talk when you're nervous.'

'I don't know anything to talk about!'

'You know enough.' He opened her wardrobe and pulled out a coat. Brown. Wondering why everything in her wardrobe was the colour of mud, he threw it towards her. 'Get dressed. We're leaving.'

'Where are we going?' Flustered, she pulled on her coat. 'Being seen with you has already got me in enough trouble. We need to separate.'

'Unfortunately it's way too late for that.'

'No, it isn't too late. All you have to do is open the front door and walk out.'

'Katie, they will crucify you.'

'I'll keep my mouth shut.' She compressed her lips and drew her fingers across in a zipping gesture. '*Silence* will be the word of the day. Except I won't say it out loud, obviously.'

Forcing aside thoughts of alternative methods of keeping her mouth occupied, Nathaniel focused on her eyes. 'As a matter of interest, what's the longest time you've gone without speaking? Not counting when you're asleep…'

'Actually, I talk in my sleep. If I'm really stressed about

something, I talk about it.' Her smile was obviously intended to be reassuring. 'But don't worry—I'm not going to sleep with any of the journalists.'

'And that's supposed to make me feel better?'

'I'm just saying you have nothing to worry about. The press aren't interested in me. I don't know any details about Annabelle or Carrie. We spent an evening together and you said nothing—just sort of glowered a lot in a brooding Heathcliff sort of way. I've never known a man say less and I've known some uncommunicative types in my time.'

'It's hard for a man to get a word in edgeways with you and, Katie, they *are* interested in you.' Intent on providing proof of that fact, Nathaniel removed his phone from his pocket and accessed the Internet with one stab of his finger. Following a hunch, he fed a series of keywords into the search engine and then clenched his jaw as the results sprang onto his screen. He held it up towards her. 'Here is an example of how *not* interested in you they are. They already have all the information on you, including name, age and your Internet dating profile.'

She stood rigid, staring at the screen. 'That's my picture,' she whispered. 'Where did they get my picture?'

'Here's another—'

'Wait a minute, when did they take that?' Snatching the phone from him, she read the headline. '*Is She the Reason Nathaniel Wolfe Walked Off the Stage Last Night?* Well, of course I'm not the reason! I rescued you! We have to tell them the truth! Go out there and tell them the truth.'

He had no intention of telling anyone the truth.

'The press aren't interested in the truth. The best we can do is absent ourselves and hope they go and hound someone else instead.'

'That isn't very nice for the someone else.'

'You'd rather they set up camp outside your flat? Stick

cameras through your letter box? Interview your neighbours? Track down every boyfriend you've ever had?'

'That would take them less than five minutes!' Her face was pale. 'I really hate having my picture taken. You have no idea how much I hate it. I don't even share photos on Facebook.'

He frowned as he saw a sheen of tears in her eyes. Accustomed to spending time with actresses and models who would run their own mother over if it meant a decent publicity shot, he found it hard to believe she was genuine. But there was no doubting the misery in her face. 'Why do you hate it?'

She dipped her head and fastened the buttons on her coat. 'I just do. And I don't see why anyone would be interested in my love life.'

'Because you're with me,' he said gently. 'People love reading about other people's scandals and misfortunes over their breakfast cereal.'

'I don't. I *hate* reading about bad stuff happening. I like happy stories. *Man Rescues Dog from Tree*—that sort of thing.'

'You're not an average person. Which gives us a problem. Pack a bag and grab your passport. You're coming with me.'

'You cannot be serious.'

'If I leave you here they'll feed on you like sharks attacking raw meat.'

'If I'm the raw meat in that analogy, then it isn't a very flattering description. No woman wants to think her thighs would provide sufficient food for one shark, let alone sharks in the plural.'

'Katie—' he stifled his exasperation '—just get your passport. Move!'

She planted her feet firmly and straightened her shoulders as if ready to repel an invading army. 'I'm not going anywhere with you. Apart from the fact I can't relax around you, I have a job, friends, family—I have a *life*.' She broke off as his phone rang. 'Tell whoever it is that they need to pick you up right now and get you out of here.'

Nathaniel checked the identity of the caller. 'It's my agent. I need to take this. Don't go anywhere. I'm going to arrange for us to be picked up.'

How long before the journalists made the connection with her famous sister?

How long before the comparisons started?

Katie paced up and down the bedroom, trying to stay calm.

Honestly, she was a grown woman, not a vulnerable teenager. She should have got over this by now.

She was who she was. Comparisons might hurt her feelings, but they wouldn't actually damage her physically. She just needed to get on with her life and hope the fuss eventually died down. Maybe she could take a sleeping bag to the theatre and camp there until this all blew over. The security guys had always been really kind to her.

Through the open door she could hear Nathaniel's cultured drawl as he issued a string of commands down the phone.

He found her sexy.

Gripped by a fit of shivering, Katie rubbed her hands up her arms.

'Nathaniel Wolfe, screen god and global sex symbol.'

Did he really find her sexy? She'd convinced herself that the chemistry was all wishful thinking on her part....

'Have you got your passport?' He was standing in the doorway, and the way he watched her with those slanting blue eyes made it impossible to think of anything but sex. Wild, crazy, animal sex—the sort she'd read about but never experienced.

Seriously unsettled, Katie turned away. 'I don't need my

passport. I'm going to go straight to the theatre and lock myself in the wardrobe department. They have security there, and—'

'You're not going back to the theatre.'

'Of course I'm going back to the theatre. I have a job to do.'

'I walked out on the opening night. The play has closed.' He delivered the news bluntly and she felt her knees wobble.

Not her job.

No.

She had a plan. *She had a dream.*

'You're s-saying I've lost my job?'

'Yes, and that's *my* fault,' Nathaniel growled, 'and if you could try not to look as though I've just killed your favourite pet, I'd appreciate it because right now we have to get out of here and it isn't going to help to be weighed down with guilt and recrimination.'

'I—I've really lost my job?'

'Yes.' The word hissed through his teeth. 'But I'll fix it.'

'How? Are you going to go back on that stage?'

'No.'

'Then you can't fix it.' The implications thudded home. 'This play was an important part of my career plan. I was going to get noticed. It was the first rung of the ladder...'

'There are other plays—'

'Do you know how many people applied for that job?' Panic drove her voice up an octave. 'Eight hundred! And it's the same for every job. You have no idea what it's like—'

'I'll give you access to my address book.'

'I don't want to make it because of who I know.'

'Then you're being naïve,' he said coldly, 'because that's what success in this business is all about.'

Trying to think straight, Katie shook her head stubbornly. 'Apart from the fact I don't have any money, I have a really important meeting today with a costume designer. It's even more important now I'm jobless.'

Jobless. The word made her want to hyperventilate. She couldn't afford to be jobless.

Nathaniel sighed. 'What's her name?'

'Meredith Beynon.'

'Never heard of her. She'll do nothing for your career.'

'But—'

'What you need is an apprenticeship with one of the top costume designers. Have you heard of Alicia Brent?'

'Of course. Everyone has. But she's not going to talk to someone like me.'

'She will if I tell her to. Good. That's settled. Now, fetch your passport. We have to get out of here.'

Katie's head was spinning. 'You know Alicia Brent?'

'Yes. And if it doesn't work out with her, there are others.' His voice had an edge to it. 'Passport!'

Suddenly her future was hazy and terrifyingly unclear. A meeting with Alicia Brent wasn't going to pay off her debts, was it? *She needed work.* 'Where are you planning to go?'

'A journalist-free zone. I need to lie low until the Sapphire ceremony. A deserted island. Sun, sea and se—'

'I am *not* having sex with you.'

A ghost of a smile touched his mouth. 'I was going to say seclusion, but sex sounds good to me. You talk when you're awake and you talk in your sleep. It remains to be seen whether you talk during sex.'

CHAPTER FOUR

WHY the hell had he brought her with him?

At the time it had seemed the only way to make sure she didn't talk to the press, but he was only now realising what her presence meant. He had company at a time when he wanted it least.

Not just company. He had Katie—a girl who believed that all would be right with the world providing you had someone with whom to share your problems. A girl who believed talking solved everything.

It was probably just punishment for dragging her into this mess.

She was furious with him.

He glanced at her tense profile, careful to reveal nothing of his own emotions.

'You don't have to look as though your world has come to an end,' he ground out. 'It was a small-time costume drama with second-rate actors. It would have been provincial and boring.'

'It was another step up the ladder.'

'How many steps does this ladder of yours have? You might want to think about taking two at a time or you're never going to reach the top.'

'Do you have to be sarcastic about everything?'

'That play would *not* have progressed your career.'

'I had some really original ideas for the costumes. My name would have been on the credits.'

'Which three people would have seen. Anyway, you'd never have got the job.'

'Thanks. So not only did you stop me going, but now you're telling me I'm rubbish at my job.' She turned her head deliberately and looked out of the window. 'Just because I don't work in Hollywood doesn't mean I don't have feelings. I think you're incredibly mean.'

'Mean?' Fighting an inexplicable urge to laugh, Nathaniel stared at the back of her head. 'I haven't heard that word since I started at boarding school.'

'I bet you were a complete nightmare at boarding school.'

'I had my moments. And for your information, I wasn't being "mean" or sarcastic, I was being honest. They wouldn't have given you the job.'

Her shoulders grew a little stiffer. 'I heard you the first time. You don't need to repeat yourself.'

'I saw the costume plot. Your drawings are in a class of their own.'

'Just because I'm not—' Her head turned. 'What did you say?'

'Your drawings are in a class of their own. You have great talent. And you would have terrified them. Your work is far too imaginative and original. They would have gone with something "safe" and predictable that has been done a thousand times before. Provincial, boring producers don't want to rock the boat.' That assessment was met with a long tense silence.

'You think I have talent? You're not just saying that because I'm angry with you?'

'I'm saying it because it's the truth.'

'Oh.' A confused frown pulled at her brows. 'Well, that's nice. Unfortunately you admiring my work won't pay my bills or help me up the ladder. Not that I expect you to understand.

You live in a world of private jets, bodyguards and limousines. I live in a world of rising debt and unemployment.'

She knew nothing about his world.

'Relax, wardrobe. I'll make some calls and get you work in Hollywood. If it doesn't work out with Alicia, then I'll call Rupert Schneider or Howard Kennington.'

Her mouth opened and closed. 'You know *all* those people?'

'Yes. And they're always on the lookout for new talent. They'd love you.'

'Y-you'd introduce me? Seriously?' She looked stunned. 'Well, thank you. It's nice to know you do, in fact, have a conscience.'

'Don't endow me with qualities I don't possess. I'm introducing you because you have talent, and because I can't stand a woman who sulks, especially if I'm stuck on an island with her.'

'You should have thought of that before you forced me to come along with you. There is such a thing as karma, you know. You'll be punished in some way for doing this to me.'

'I'm already being punished. I'm about to be trapped on an island with a woman who can't stop talking. Man's idea of hell, believe me.' Smiling, Nathaniel leaned back against the seat and closed his eyes. Immediately, reality closed in and his thoughts turned dark. He saw Jacob sitting in the front row. Saw those dark eyes looking at him. Knowing. They were bound together by the past. Nothing was ever going to change that.

His smile faded and his eyes flew open.

Oh, yes, he was being punished.

'Are you all right?' Katie's big green eyes were full of concern. 'Only you're gripping your seat really hard.'

Nathaniel released his grip and the blood flowed back into his fingers. 'I'm a nervous flyer.'

'You flew a plane in your last film. You have a pilot's licence.'

'Precisely.' He hauled in all of his professional skills to make sure he didn't falter. 'I hate being flown by someone else. I'd rather be the one at the controls but I had a lousy night's sleep on your lumpy sofa and I didn't want to crash us into a mountain.'

Her steady gaze suggested that she wasn't convinced and he reminded himself that Katie Field noticed things. He couldn't afford to lower his guard. Which suited him just fine. Apart from last night, onstage, Nathaniel couldn't remember the last time he'd lowered his guard.

'So this island—' The hope of new contacts seemed to have cheered her slightly. 'Where is it? And how do you know we won't be followed around when we get there?'

'It's a tropical island off the coast of South America. And the reason I know we won't be followed around is because we'll be the only two people on the island.'

'Just us?' Her voice was a horrified squeak. 'You expect me to spend two weeks without a single person to talk to?'

'I believe there are two species of parrot found on the island. If you play your cards right, one of them might talk to you.'

'You may think you're funny, but I'm the sort of person who likes company. If you're the only person on the island—' her eyes narrowed '—then I'll just have to talk to you.'

'Talk away. Just don't expect me to answer.' Nathaniel watched her through the dark shield of his lashes. 'On the other hand, if it's company you want, I'm sure we can find some way of passing the time that doesn't include conversation.'

He was arrogant, overbearing—Katie sighed. *And insanely sexy.*

How could he be sexy when he was asleep? Strands of dark hair flopped over his forehead giving him a dangerous, rakish look. The bold black brows and darkened jaw were wholly masculine and as for that mouth—

She looked away quickly, her heart thudding against her chest.

No, no, no.

She wasn't going to do that to herself. Not again. No more fantasies about unobtainable guys. She knew who she was now and was comfortable with herself. Five minutes of idle flirtation with a hot movie star didn't change anything.

Blind with tiredness but totally unable to relax enough to sleep, Katie stared out of the window at the tropical islands that studded the sparkling ocean below.

Some of the tiredness sloughed away as she gazed beneath her. The sea was dotted with emerald-green islands, each framed by white sands and coral reefs. Clear turquoise water lapped at secluded coves. *Paradise*, she thought, *with a twist.*

She sneaked a glance at Nathaniel, sleeping beside her.

He was the twist.

What secrets was he hiding? Who were Annabelle and Carrie? Why did he feel the need to bury himself on a deserted island?

The questions spiralled in her head until sheer exhaustion made her fall asleep. When she woke it was to find Nathaniel staring out of the window.

For a few seconds she saw torment and anguish in his eyes and then he realised she was awake and quickly blanked it.

What was going on in his life? *What was he hiding?* 'Have we arrived?'

'We're in Rio de Janeiro. It's a short helicopter hop to Wolfe Island.'

'This island—' she retrieved her bag from under her seat '—you said your brother owns it?'

'He's a hotelier. Very convenient at times like this.'

'Wolfe.' Katie stared at him for a moment, wondering how

she could have failed to make the connection. 'Sebastian Wolfe is your brother?'

'That's right.'

'I've heard of him, of course. I just hadn't realised—you never talk about your family.'

'And I don't intend to start.'

'You're not close to your family?'

A muscle flickered at the corner of his mouth. 'You certainly like to live dangerously.'

'If we're going to be trapped together for the next two weeks we have to know a few things about each other.'

Those sexy, slanting eyes were faintly mocking. 'You need to know I'm dangerous when I'm cross-examined.'

'And I'm dangerous when I'm deprived of human conversation. I'm not cross-examining you. I'm just asking about your family. I don't see what's wrong with that. I'm just being polite.'

'Let's set some ground rules, shall we?' Thick dark lashes swept down to conceal his expression. 'You don't ask me anything personal and I won't ask you anything personal. In fact, why don't we just agree to a no-talking rule for the next two weeks? It's fine with me if we keep our relationship purely physical. We can communicate via body language.'

Katie chose to ignore that. 'You can ask me anything you like. I don't have secrets. And I can't not talk for two weeks. Talking is how I relieve tension.'

He leaned towards her, his blue eyes two narrow, dangerous slits of simmering sensuality. 'Want to know how I relieve tension, wardrobe?'

'No, I do not.' Trapped by his gaze, she found it hard to breathe. He was a man who clearly understood the effect he had on women.

As if to confirm that, his smile was slow and confident. 'Sure?'

'Completely sure.'

'But you're curious.' His voice was soft and seductive. 'Admit it—you've been wondering how it is going to feel when we eventually stop all this self-control nonsense and kiss each other.'

'I haven't. It hasn't crossed my mind.'

'You're a terrible liar.'

'And you're impossibly arrogant. And arrogance,' she said breathlessly, 'is never an attractive trait, even for the Sexiest Man Alive.' Her heart was pounding and the blood hummed in her ears.

'You think I'm the sexiest man alive?'

'I was quoting opinion polls.' Thoroughly flustered, Katie looked out of the window again. 'We're landing.' *Thank goodness.* How come he always knew what to say and she never did? How come he never seemed to feel awkward?

He unbuckled his seat belt and leaned across to do hers. 'Let's move. The helicopter is waiting.'

The first thing that hit her when she stepped out onto the island was the intense heat and the colours. Deep green palm trees shaded milky white sand, and a parrot added a flash of exotic red as it took refuge in the trees clustered in the centre of the island. The hot sun was a ball of orange and the sea was a magic carpet of glittering jewelled blue.

'Beats London in February.' Nathaniel took her arm and drew her away from the helicopter. 'Here we are. Home sweet home. Otherwise known as Paradise Villa. All the bedrooms open onto the terrace and overlook the sea. Take your pick.'

Feeling hot and sticky in her jeans, Katie walked into the house and stopped dead, stunned by what she saw. 'Oh, it's—'

'Yes. My brother has flawless taste. It's the jewel in his company crown. VIP all the way.'

Katie gazed around her. The outdoor living area was cleverly designed to offer maximum shade while making the most of the breathtaking views. Exotic plants swayed lazily in the breeze and deep cream sofas invited relaxation and indulgence. The only sound was the swish of the sea as it rushed onto the sand. It was another world. 'Who can afford to stay here?'

'We can.' Nathaniel urged her forward. 'Most of the living space is outdoors, obviously, because of the view. Terrace, infinity pool, hammocks—you'll find everything you need to chill out and do nothing. If you get bored doing nothing, there are water sports.'

Katie felt faint. 'So when people come here, they book the whole island?'

'Indeed they do. They come here for peace and quiet and to experience the unique challenges of having hot sweaty sex in a hammock.' His smile was slow and sexy. 'You've never tried sex in a hammock?'

'You're not funny.' Feeling as though she'd been plunged into a furnace, Katie pulled off her jumper. 'Is there somewhere I can buy some clothes? Next time you kidnap someone, warn them to pack for hot weather. I'm boiling to death wearing jeans in this heat.' Or maybe it wasn't the heat. *Maybe it was him…*

That disturbing blue gaze was slumberous. 'The staff were instructed to put some clothes in your room.'

Great. Her worst nightmare. Someone else choosing her clothes.

Speculating on the sort of woman the staff would have expected to see with Nathaniel Wolfe and sensing major embarrassment, Katie's heart sank. She'd rather wear jeans and risk heatstroke. 'I can tell you now that nothing will fit.'

'If nothing fits, then you can walk around naked.'

'You're still not funny.' Lifting her chin, Katie walked across the terrace and back into the villa. 'I presume the bedrooms are this way?'

'That's the master suite. Unless you want to share it with me, you need to turn left.'

Katie turned left so sharply she almost fell over.

The door to another bedroom suite was open and she escaped inside, her eyebrows lifting as she saw the rose petals sprinkled on the white silk bedcover and the candles clustered around bowls of scented flowers.

It was a room for romance. A room for loving.

'Miss Katie?' A smiling woman ambled slowly into the room carrying soft fluffy towels. 'I'm Rosa, and if there's anything you need during your stay, you just have to ask.'

Katie frowned, confused. 'I thought— He said we were on our own.'

Rosa laughed, her smooth brown face alight with amusement. 'Bless you. This place has a staff of twenty. But we all live on the mainland. We arrive in time to make breakfast and leave after supper. So you have the best of both worlds. I arranged for some clothes for you, but if they're not right just let me know.'

They were going to be too tight, all the wrong colours and it was going to be hideously embarrassing. But Katie was too polite to complain. 'I'm sure they'll be perfect. Thanks very much.'

Perfect or not, it was a relief to peel off her jeans. After a deliciously cool shower in a luxurious bathroom with one side open to the beach, she wrapped herself in a soft fluffy white towel and wandered into the walk-in closet. *Oh, to live like this.* An array of colourful bikinis had been spread out for her and she gave them a single horrified glance and reached for a primrose sundress. Yellow was too bold a colour for her, but it was better than squeezing into a bikini in front of Nathaniel Wolfe.

She slipped on the dress, relieved to find it fitted perfectly. It was extremely pretty—in fact, the only thing wrong with it was the colour. It was so *bright.* And she never wore bright clothes. She preferred to blend into the background.

With a short laugh, Katie looked in the mirror and shook her head.

No chance of blending in dressed in yellow. Slipping her feet into a pair of pretty flip-flops, she walked back onto the terrace feeling as conspicuous as a sunflower in a vegetable patch.

Nathaniel had stripped off his shirt and was sprawled unselfconsciously on the white sun lounger in nothing but a pair of low-slung board shorts that showed off his rippling abs. 'It's going to be hard to swim in a dress, wardrobe.'

Feeling about as appetising as a piece of uncooked pasta, Katie sat down neatly on the sun lounger furthest away from him. 'I'm not swimming.' *Strip almost naked and parade in front of a man who was fed a daily diet of size-zero women?* Please.

He glanced up from his phone. 'You can't swim?'

'I can swim if I want to. I don't want to.'

'Why not? Swimming is the only way to stay cool.'

Katie slid off her sandals. 'Actually, I'm not hot.'

A sardonic smile touched the corners of his mouth. 'You look hot to me.' Leaving that ambiguous comment floating in the air, he leaned across and passed her a glass of chilled lemonade. 'What was wrong with the selection of bikinis Rosa bought you?'

'Nothing was wrong with them.'

'Then why aren't you wearing one of them?'

Abandoning subtlety in favour of honesty, Katie glared at him. 'Because there is no way I'm wearing a bikini in front of you!'

'Why not?'

'Is that a serious question?' Judging from his blank expression, she decided it was. 'Nathaniel, there are basically two types of women—the padded version and the unpadded version. You hang out with the unpadded version. I'm the padded version. You've probably never met one of me before.'

'The padded version?'

'I'm designed with extra cushioning,' she muttered, 'built for comfort, not speed. And now can we please talk about something else?'

'That's why you won't wear the bikini?' A slow smile spread across his face. 'Because you're worried about your body?'

'Call me vain, but I don't want to spend the whole day sucking in my stomach.'

'So don't.' Smiling, he leaned back against the lounger and closed his eyes. 'Women have such a distorted view of what a guy finds sexy. If the rest of you is anything to go by, I'm sure you have a very sexy stomach. Put the bikini on, and I'll give you my verdict.'

Her gaze drifted to his wide shoulders and hard chest. He had the body of a man who lived a physical life. 'I'd rather boil alive than let you see my stomach.'

'Sweetheart, if you're going to spend two weeks on a tropical island, fully clothed, then you *will* boil alive.' The fact that he was laughing at her doubled her tension.

'Don't make fun of me.'

'For what it's worth, I think you're extremely pretty,' he drawled, 'so all this insecurity about yourself is misplaced.'

'Nathaniel, I saw your leading lady in *Alpha Man*. She was a sex goddess.'

'She was a spoiled princess with a vicious temper.'

Katie remembered the high-octane sex scenes that had held the entire audience gripped. 'You didn't seem to mind her too much on screen. I seem to remember that the chemistry between you was described as "superexplosive."'

'I'm an actor.' His tone was flat. 'It's what I do.'

'Kissing the most beautiful women in the world? Tough job.'

'It can be.'

And he was acting now. She didn't think for a moment

that the man lounging across from her was the real Nathaniel Wolfe. 'So how does it work, preparing for a part like that? Did you have extra training for the part of Alpha Man?'

'I spent two months with the Special Forces.'

'You ran around the countryside with a big pack on your back?'

'Amongst other things.'

She could imagine him, hair cropped short, pushing himself to the limits. Nathaniel Wolfe, bad boy. 'Which Special Forces? U.S. or the UK?'

'If I told you that I'd have to kill you.' He spoke with that light, mocking tone that made her stomach curl. 'Let's just say it was the only time I've never been bothered by the press. Those guys are the definitive alpha man. And they're a team. Better than any family.' Something in his voice made her glance towards him but his profile revealed nothing.

Better than family.

Apart from briefly mentioning his brother Sebastian, he'd already banned that topic, hadn't he? 'You're not the only one with a complicated family. When Dad died and I discovered all his gambling debts—to start with I was so upset. And angry. I couldn't believe he'd led this whole secret life. I kept thinking of all those years Mum had kept it to herself—we had no money as kids and twice we lost our home.'

Nathaniel tilted his head. 'So basically we agree that families suck.'

Katie thought about her sister. About the way she'd divorced herself from her family.

'I don't think families suck.' She dragged her eyes from his mouth, horrified to find herself thinking about sex. Again. 'But sometimes they're messy. I still think you should stick together. Is your brother older than you?'

His gaze was watchful. 'If you don't want to end up in the pool, you should change the subject.'

'Sorry. I'm not used to having banned topics of conversation.

I'll try and talk about the weather. Or the gardens. This place is truly beautiful.' Katie looked around her and saw a mesh of palm trees and foliage, the green broken up by splashes of bright tropical colour. Spotting a large green gecko basking in the sun by the pool, she reached in her bag for a sketchbook.

'You're drawing him?'

'Why not? He's lovely.' Her pencil flew over the page and she took out a box of pastels and played with colour combinations. 'I love the mix of turquoise and tropical green. Those colours would be gorgeous in silk.' She narrowed her eyes, imagining it, spinning designs in her head.

'If you like colours so much, why do you always wear brown.'

Her pencil stilled. 'I like brown.' *And she was invisible in brown.* Katie tightened her grip on the pencil. Just holding it soothed her. 'I still love the feel of my pencil. It reminds me of when I was a child. I used to watch all the Hollywood movies and redesign the costumes.'

He locked his arms behind his head. Muscles rippled. 'Favourite movie of all time?'

'Gone with the Wind.' She kept her eyes on her sketch pad and not on those muscles. 'Fabulous costumes and so romantic. What about you? I guess it's *Alpha Man*.'

'I never watch my own movies.' Dropping his arms, he leaned across and looked at her drawing. 'I love the old Hitchcock films. *The 39 Steps* and *Notorious*—Cary Grant. One of the greatest actors never to win a Sapphire.'

'Does it mean that much? Winning a Sapphire?'

His answer was to spring to his feet and dive into the pool.

Katie put down the pencil, feeling guilty

She shouldn't ask him anything personal. It wasn't as if they knew each other. They were just two strangers trapped together by unfortunate circumstances. And yet, after the emotion she'd witnessed at the theatre and in her flat, she felt as though she did know him. She knew little bits—Annabelle, Carrie—small pieces of a jigsaw that meant nothing because there was no picture.

Frustrated, she watched as he cooled off in the pool. The sweat prickled her back. The sundress felt like a coat but there was no way she was removing it.

The initial euphoria at finding herself in paradise, dimmed. It was only paradise if you could afford the time off. She couldn't. If she couldn't find herself another job fast, she wouldn't be able to pay the mortgage. Her career would stall. Her dream would die.

And she wasn't prepared to give up on her dream.

By the time Nathaniel pulled himself out of the pool her stress levels had reached breaking point. 'Does this place have Internet access?'

He reached for a towel and dried his face. 'Why?'

'I need to look for a job. You said you'd introduce me to costume designers, but I don't see how you can do that when we're here. I need to do some job hunting.'

'Wait there.' Without enlightening her as to his intentions, he strolled into the villa. Moments later he emerged carrying a thick sheaf of papers held together by an elastic band. He dropped it into her lap. 'Read that. It's the script for my next movie. I'm finalising the funding soon. We haven't chosen a costume designer yet.'

Katie stared at the sheets of paper, looking for the meaning behind the gesture. He felt guilty? No, Nathaniel Wolfe didn't do guilt. Then why? Just to shut her up, she decided. To give her something to occupy her so that he didn't have to spend time with her. 'There's no way you'd give it to someone like me.'

'Do me some sketches and we'll talk.'

She kept the hope ruthlessly in check. 'Because your conscience is pricking you and you feel guilty that you lost me my job?'

'I've already told you, when it comes to my work, I don't have a conscience.' Without a flicker of regret or apology, he confirmed her own thoughts on that topic. 'I pick the best person for the job. I liked the drawings I saw in your flat. The question is, can you do it again with a contemporary script? This isn't Shakespeare.'

He liked her drawings enough to give her a chance? 'Are you acting or directing?'

'Directing. Don't think about actors when you read it—just think about the characters.'

'So are you giving up film acting?' Refusing to be intimidated by his silence, she tightened her fingers on the wedge of papers in her lap. 'Was that why you agreed to a stint on the stage in London?'

'Don't you ever stop asking questions?'

'Sorry. I'm not good with silences. I'm trying to be polite.'

'We're not at a palace garden party.' His soft drawl brushed over her nerve endings and Katie looked at him.

'You're not the only one finding this situation difficult. You could be a little more friendly.' And a little less intimidating. A little less masculine. A little less…everything.

The smile that tugged the corners of his mouth definitely wasn't friendly. It was dangerous. 'Change into a bikini and I'll show you how friendly I can be.'

He was just baiting her, she knew that. He couldn't possibly be serious. A man who had his pick of women wasn't ever going to pick her.

Katie thought about her sister's perfect bone structure and endless legs. Next to Paula, she'd never felt anything but depressingly ordinary and a man like Nathaniel Wolfe was never going to be interested in ordinary.

Her fingers tightened around the bunch of papers. 'How long until dinner?'

If he wasn't going to talk, she might as well read the script.

Nathaniel waited impatiently, his fingers strumming a rhythm on the table. Two messages sat unopened on his phone, both from Jacob.

His temper and his mood simmered along at one degree under boiling point. Even on the other side of the world, his past hunted him. 'Did Katie say how long she would be?'

'I knocked on her door but there was no answer. I thought she might have been asleep. You had a long flight.' Ben poured chilled wine into a glass. 'You want me to call her again?'

'I'll do it myself.' Desperate for distraction, Nathaniel left the phone on the table and strode back inside the villa towards the guest suite. The door was shut. He tapped once and received no answer so he opened the door and walked in.

And stopped dead.

Katie lay on her stomach on the bed, dressed only in a skimpy lace plunge bra and an equally skimpy thong, both in the same shade of hot pink. The headphones from her bright pink iPod trailed from her ears and she lay with her chin on her hand, completely absorbed by the script. Her head bobbed in time to the music and occasionally she made a little sketch in the margin.

Nathaniel's mind blanked. He forgot about the texts waiting for him on his phone. Instead he stood still, transfixed by the creamy curve of her bottom revealed by the thong. He remembered the lacy camisole she'd worn to bed. Nothing about the way she dressed hinted at a secret love of sexy underwear. *Underneath all that boring brown she'd been wearing hot pink lacy silk?*

Engulfed by a scorching flame of lust, he felt himself harden. Dinner, he decided, was going to be delayed.

Kicking the door shut behind him, Nathaniel strolled into the room just as she glanced up and saw him there.

With a squeak of horror, she yanked the earphones out of her ears and scrambled off the bed, scattering pages of the script over the floor.

'Get out of here!' Her scarlet face clashing with the hot pink underwear, she grabbed the dress she'd been wearing earlier and clutched it to her chest, but not before Nathaniel had been treated to a full frontal display of her generous curves.

'Just for the record, you definitely don't need to suck in your stomach,' he drawled. 'And I thoroughly approve of the underwear.'

'Don't you *knock*?'

'I knocked. You weren't listening.'

'I was reading—'

'In your underwear?'

'I was *hot*.'

'Now, *that* we can agree on.' Nathaniel delivered a smile of undiluted masculine approval. 'Why do you always wear brown on the outside when you've got all that lacy pink going on underneath?'

Her green eyes flashed a warning. If he'd been keen on the safe route he would have left the room, but Nathaniel had always preferred to live dangerously so he strolled towards her, prised the dress from her rigid fingers and studied the smooth perfection of her soft curves. 'You have an incredible body.'

'Get out of here!'

He discovered that playing with fire distracted him from all the things he didn't want to be thinking about. 'Of all the secrets you've spilled in the past twenty-four hours, this one is definitely the best.' He tumbled her back onto the bed, pinning her arms as she tried to roll.

'What are you doing?'

'You said you wanted to get to know me better. This is the

quickest way I know.' Without thinking he brought his mouth down on hers, capturing her soft lips with his, smothering her moan of shock. Her mouth opened and he tasted the sweetness and then desire slammed into him, the explosion of need consuming him like a fever. Nathaniel locked his hand in her hair and plundered that mouth, turning what had begun as an experiment into a kiss of such erotic intensity that the shock of it exploded right through his body. Sucked under by the sheer impact of raw physical chemistry, he slid his hand under the smooth curve of her bottom, bringing her into contact with the urgent thrust of his arousal. His need for her desperate, he teased her lower lip with his teeth and tongue and then lowered his mouth to her breast. Pink lacy fabric acted as a barrier between them and he dragged it aside with impatient fingers and fastened his mouth around one thrusting peak—and tasted heaven.

He heard the sudden snatch of her breath and felt her fingers dig hard into his shoulders. When he skimmed her breasts with tongue and fingers, she moaned under him, the sensuous movement of her hips unleashing a ravenous hunger inside him.

Nathaniel lost all sense of time and place.

His brain shut down and he responded with pure animal instinct.

Sliding his hand between her legs, he breached the barrier of her underwear and explored her slick softness with bold, gentle fingers. He felt her stiffen beneath him and then she shoved hard at his chest.

'No.'

He heard her through a dark mist of ferocious, primal need.

'Nathaniel, no—'

It was the tone that registered, rather than the words. That and the sharp bite of her nails in his shoulders.

Lifting his head, he stared into green eyes glazed with the

same need that tore through him. He tried to speak but there was only one part of him that seemed to be working. Nathaniel licked his lips, realising that he hadn't just found distraction, he'd found oblivion.

Shaken by his own lack of control, he rolled away from her. 'Sorry,' he drawled. 'Blame it on the padding. For the record, it's in all the right places.'

What had happened to him?

Seriously unsettled, he stared up at the canopy that draped the four-poster bed in soft creamy folds. *Romance*, he thought. The whole damn room was designed for romance and happy endings. And there wasn't a happy ending within a million miles of him.

Nathaniel sprang to his feet and strolled towards the door. 'I came to tell you dinner is served.'

'Nathaniel—'

Behind him, he could hear the rustle of fabric as she pulled on her dress. He didn't turn. Because he didn't know what had happened, he couldn't be sure it wouldn't happen again.

His hand on the door handle, he gave a smile of self-mockery. 'I'll see you on the terrace, wardrobe.'

'Nathaniel, for goodness' sake, wait!' There was a soft thud as her feet hit the floor. 'You can't just—We nearly— Damn it, do you ever talk about *anything*?'

Not if he could help it. He turned to look at her and then wished he hadn't because her hair was mussed and sexy and her mouth was softly bruised from his kisses.

'Do you have to talk about *everything*?'

'Not everything—' she looked confused, exasperated '—but you just…we just—'

'But we didn't.' Nathaniel opened the door. 'You said no. I stopped. End of conversation.'

'No, it isn't the end of the conversation!' She stalked over to him. '*Why* did you kiss me?'

'You were lying semi-naked in provocative underwear on an enormous bed.'

'So your criteria for having sex with someone is that you like their underwear. Don't you ever want to get to know someone?'

No, never.

Nathaniel took advantage of the open door. 'Dinner,' he murmured, 'is definitely served.'

CHAPTER FIVE

KATIE felt dizzy and light-headed, as if her body might float off at any moment.

It didn't help to tell herself that his job had taught him how to make a kiss hot and seductive and how to make a woman feel irresistible. Nor did it help to remind herself that she'd been half naked, which was sufficient provocation for a red-blooded male like Nathaniel Wolfe.

In fact, nothing helped.

She still felt…desirable.

Sneaking a look at him through the flickering candles that lit the dinner table, she saw that he was staring at a point in the distance, his dark brows locked in a brooding frown.

Unobserved, Katie looked at his mouth. How many times had she watched him on the big screen and wondered how it would feel to be kissed by him?

Now she had her answer. *It felt incredible.*

She had to remind herself it wasn't real. If she fooled herself that he'd been carried away by passion, then she'd be forgetting her own theories. He was an actor. He could play any part he chose.

Awkward with the extended silence, she spoke. 'I read the play….'

'Play?' His blank look made her realise how distracted he was.

'Your play.'

'Right.' His face cleared. 'If you were gripped enough to read it in your knickers, presumably you liked it. Any ideas?'

Determined not to show him how much that one kiss had flustered her, Katie beamed at Ben as he served chargrilled vegetables. 'Yum. That looks delicious, thanks. You spoil me.'

Ben returned the smile. 'I'll be hovering right here if there's anything you need, Miss Katie.'

'No, you won't.' Nathaniel's voice was silky smooth. 'If we need anything, we'll call you.'

As Ben discreetly melted away, Katie rolled her eyes and picked up her fork. 'Do people always do exactly what you want?'

'Evidently not,' he purred, 'or right now you would be naked on that bed underneath me and we'd be indulging in a form of communication that certainly doesn't require conversation.'

'There's nothing wrong with conversation.'

'Fine. So let's talk. Tell me why you always wear brown.'

'I happen to like the colour brown.'

He leaned forward, his gaze disturbingly acute. 'Why don't you like having your picture taken?'

'Not everyone is born an exhibitionist.'

'Here's a hint—' he spoke softly '—when you're lying, you need to look someone in the eye and act sincere. You, Katie Field, are an appalling liar. And you have your secrets, just like anyone else.' He lifted his glass and took a mouthful of wine, watching her over the rim of his glass.

Not secrets, she thought. Insecurities. It wasn't the same thing.

Their eyes held and she felt the blood pound in her ears.

But *he* had secrets, that much was obvious. And she suspected they were dark secrets. Secrets he didn't share with anyone.

What surprised her was how much she wanted him to share them.

How much she wanted to provide a listening ear.

He was looking at her with those spectacular eyes and suddenly talking and listening were the last things on her mind. It was obvious that he was thinking about that kiss. And so was she.

Her pulse thudding dangerously fast, Katie put down her fork. Seeking a safe subject, she chose acting. 'Tell me more about how you prepared for the part of Alpha Man.'

She half expected him to refuse, but he relaxed back in his chair and proceeded to regale her with stories about filming. He was witty and sharp, his observations about his cast members so wickedly incisive that she found herself laughing even though she'd promised herself she wasn't going to fall under his spell.

He was such amusing company that it was only after the last of the plates had been cleared away that she realised he still hadn't revealed anything personal. The whole evening had been spent talking about other people.

'So, how about you, little Miss Talkalot.' He leaned across and topped up her wine glass. 'How did you end up designing costumes? School play?'

Make me something to wear, Katie.

'Way before the school play.' She dismissed her sister's petulant voice from her head. 'I always loved costumes. Clothes. I used to make my own dolls' clothes. We didn't have that much money so I used scraps of fabric and old buttons from Mum's sewing kit. I hovered around thrift stores, car boot sales—anything I could find. My friends and I used to play Hollywood.' Afraid she was boring him to death, she broke off and took a sip of her drink.

'You used to *play* Hollywood?'

'We'd pretend we were a film studio. Martha was the director.' Katie grinned at the memory. 'She was the bossy one. Then there was Emily—she was the drama queen so she always had the leading part. Sally and Jenny took whichever parts Emily didn't want.' And then there was her sister, Paula. *I have to be the princess. I'm the prettiest.*

'And you?'

'I made everyone else look good.' She gave a simple shrug. 'All I ever did at school was draw and draw. We had a school prom and I designed and made everyone's dresses. My parents wanted me to read English at university, but all I was interested in was art, fashion, the movies and theatre. That's all I ever wanted to do and they were so good about it. Were your parents good about you wanting to be an actor?'

'I never asked their opinion.' His face was inscrutable.

'I read somewhere that you left home at sixteen and went to Hollywood. That's pretty young. My parents would have totally freaked out if I'd suggested crossing the Atlantic at that age.'

'I had an opportunity. I took it.'

'And your parents didn't try and talk you out of it? Lucky you. I did my degree in London and my mum and dad were constantly worried about what would happen to me. Not that I'm complaining,' Katie said hastily, 'because at the end of the day you know it's because they care. Yours were obviously pretty chilled about that sort of stuff.'

His eyes glittered and he rose to his feet. 'Goodnight, Katie.'

'Oh, but I—' Her mouth opened and closed because she was talking to herself. Nathaniel had gone.

Katie spent the next few days poring over the script and making sketches.

She saw virtually nothing of Nathaniel.

After that first night, he'd kept his distance. They ate meals together and when he talked about films he'd made he was entertaining company, but she was acutely aware that he was acting a part. The part of host. He said nothing about himself and his conversation was delivered with the same air of bored mockery that characterised all his communication. The slightest attempt on her part to turn their verbal exchanges into something more personal was met by an impenetrable icy wall.

Increasingly lonely, Katie took to hanging out with the staff. She befriended Ben and even went out fishing with him early one morning. She spent time with Sylvia and Kylie who cooked for them. Soon she was firm friends with everyone.

Everyone except Nathaniel.

'You talked to Ben for so long today he couldn't get his work done,' Nathaniel drawled one evening as they ate a delicious meal.

Katie put down her fork, trying not to feel hurt. 'We were chatting. Do you know he only gets to see his girlfriend once a week?'

'Lucky guy.' Nathaniel suppressed a yawn. 'He gets the sex and none of the rest of the junk that comes with a relationship.'

'Do you always have to be sarcastic about everything?'

'Who says I'm being sarcastic?'

Katie thought about his wicked reputation with women. 'Haven't you ever been in love?'

He threw back his head and laughed, genuinely amused. 'That's a question straight from Katie-land where the sky is blue and the sun always shines.'

Angry, she stood quickly, knocking over her chair in the process. 'Actually, the sky isn't that blue in Katie-land. I've had my share of problems. My life has bumps in it, just like anyone's. Right now I've lost my job, thanks to you, and there is no way any bank is going to give me another loan when

I don't have work. Not that I expect someone like you to understand.'

'So if it's raining in Katie-land,' he said softly, 'why are you always so damned cheerful?'

Katie picked the chair up and sat down on it slowly. 'I don't know.' She bit her lip. 'I suppose I just prefer being happy to being miserable. Over the years I've learned what cheers me up.'

'Talking?'

'Yes—' she flushed '—I like people. I find people interesting and generally very warm and friendly. Human contact is what makes life OK when things are tough.'

'Really? Generally I find it to be the other way round.' His beautiful mouth curled. 'Human beings are what make life tough when things are OK. I presume your need to talk and make friends is the reason you're distracting all the staff.'

'I'm not distracting them.'

'Sweetheart, you're virtually on the payroll.'

'I'd love to be on the payroll! At least then I'd be earning some money. And it's better than being lonely by the pool.'

'Lonely?' Black eyebrows rose in incredulous surprise. 'How can you possibly be lonely? You're in paradise.'

'It's only paradise if you have someone to share it with. What's the point of spotting a gorgeous bird if you don't have anyone to get excited with.' Katie poked at her food. 'Today I was reduced to having a long conversation with a lizard.'

'I saw one unconscious on the path,' he drawled, deadpan. 'Now I know why. He'd been "Katied."'

'You think it's funny, but I happen to like talking to people.'

'I had no idea you were lonely. I thought you were working on my script.'

'I am, but I work better when I have people around me. My creativity is totally stifled otherwise.'

'You can talk to me.'

'You're hardly ever around. You avoid all conversation. You're no fun.'

A slow, dangerous smile touched his mouth. 'Any time you want me to demonstrate how much fun I can be, just let me know.'

'I don't mean that sort of fun.' Her heart galloped off at a frantic pace. 'I mean the sort of fun you can have just talking to someone—' She broke off as his phone buzzed. 'Aren't you going to answer that?'

'No.' He leaned towards her, those impossibly thick lashes shielding his gorgeous eyes. 'There's more fun to be had by not talking to someone.'

Why was he ignoring his phone?

'Stop playing games.' Katie wiped damp palms over her shorts. 'If we had sex, you'd really hurt me.'

'I promise to keep my caveman tendencies under control and be incredibly gentle.'

Her mouth dried and her cheeks flamed. 'I didn't mean it like that.'

'I know what you meant.' He leaned back in his chair. 'Wicked, bad Nathaniel would bring thunderstorms to Katie-land. It could end in serious flooding.'

'You're mocking me, as usual, but I'd rather be optimistic than a cynic like you.'

His phone started to ring again but he continued to ignore it and stood. 'I'm sorry I've neglected you.' He held out his hand. 'I'm sorry I've been in a vile mood. Let's walk on the beach. You haven't lived until you've seen a sunset on Wolfe Island.'

Her gaze flickered to the phone, abandoned on the table. 'Don't you think you should see who was ringing? It might be important.'

His fingers closed over hers, warm and strong. 'Not as important as seeing a sunset.'

'I'd love to see the sunset, but...' With a final glance at the phone, she followed him down onto the soft, white sand that curved below the villa, telling herself that it wasn't her business if he ignored his calls. Enjoying the beach, she stooped to pick up a shell. 'I never imagined that anywhere as idyllic as this existed. How often do you come here?'

'Whenever I need privacy.'

Katie curled her toes into the sand, loving the warmth and the softness. 'It's lucky your brother owns it. It's a great place for family gatherings.'

'When I come here, it's for solitude.'

So he didn't come here with his family. Deciding that she'd better keep her mouth shut on that subject, Katie walked in silence, clamping her lips together whenever she had the urge to speak.

When they reached some large boulders that protected the next beach, he put out his hand to help her over. 'The best view on the island is from here.' He vaulted over the last rock with athletic grace and stood, powerful and strong, staring over the sea. 'This is Turtle Cove.'

'It's beautiful.' Slinging her bag down on the sand, Katie sat and rested her chin on her knees. 'I did some preliminary sketches for your script, by the way. Just a few ideas. Might be completely wrong and not what you were imagining.'

'Do you have them with you?'

She reached into her bag and pulled out her pad, suddenly nervous. 'They're just ideas.'

He sat down next to her and took her sketch pad. Silent, he flipped through the pages. 'Brown?'

'Yes, because in this scene she isn't sure of herself. She doesn't want to stand out. Then later—' Katie leaned across and turned another page '—here, she's wearing bolder, more flamboyant colours and everything is tailored because she isn't hiding behind her clothes any more.' Suddenly she realised what she'd done and she felt a flash of mortification.

She'd made it personal. 'If you don't think it's a good idea I can—'

'I think it's a great idea. I wouldn't have thought of doing it like that. You've shown her character arc through costume.' Nathaniel studied the drawings carefully. If he spotted any parallels, he didn't comment. 'They're original. Clever.'

'You really like them?'

'Yes. Can you work up a costume plot?'

'Do you have a computer I can use?'

'You can't do it the old-fashioned way with pen and paper?'

'Yes, but it won't look so professional and you won't be able to email it to whoever you need to email it to.'

'Good point. I'll sort something out for you.' He sprang to his feet and held out his hand. 'Sun's going down. If you want romantic, this is the closest you'll get.'

She didn't want romantic, did she? At least, not with this man. She wasn't that foolish. But after a moment's hesitation she took his hand and let him pull her upright. The chemistry sparked immediately.

She knew he felt it too, because she heard him swear under his breath.

For a moment she thought he was going to ignore the heat, but then he hauled her into him and the searing burn of his mouth on hers melted the last of her inhibitions. Flames licked at her nerve endings and a wicked thrill shot through her entire body. She felt his hand slide to the base of her back and he pulled her hard against him, his other hand locked in the soft mass of her hair as he used his mouth with erotic purpose.

His fingers massaged her scalp, his touch so inherently sexual that her excitement levels shot into overload.

Her eyes flew open and she found herself staring straight into his.

In that single moment she saw Alpha Man, the ruthless soldier about to possess the daughter of his enemy.

Confused by that vision, Katie pulled her mouth from his. 'No.' It was hard to breathe. 'This is…surreal. I look at you and I see the movie star, not the man.'

He lowered his forehead to hers. 'You just kissed the man, Katie.'

She dragged herself out of his arms, and stepped backwards, the sand warm and soft under her feet. 'I just assume you're acting. Like earlier in the week—'

'I wasn't acting then and I'm not acting now.'

Of course he was acting. He could act desire every bit as convincingly as he could act daring and dangerous. 'You know how to look at a woman in a way that makes her feel beautiful. The scary thing is I *know* that, but it still works on me.'

'Katie—'

'And much as I'd love to tell myself that I'm stunning enough to attract the world's sexiest movie star, one look in the mirror reminds me that I'm not. You can look at a woman like that and not mean it, I know you can. You do it on the screen all the time. When you kissed the daughter of your enemy in *Alpha Man* you were so convincing that I actually believed that the two of you must be together in real life because I just couldn't imagine how you could look at her like that and not mean it.'

'I've already told you I couldn't stand the woman.'

'I know.' Katie gave a confused laugh. 'Which shows how good an actor you are! And that proves my point.' She ran her tongue over her lips, wishing she'd never let him kiss her. Now she just wanted more and she knew that if she allowed herself more she'd be in dangerous territory. Whatever she shared with this man would be scorching and intense, but it would also be fleeting and ultimately painful. 'You made me come here because you were worried I'd talk to the press, so I'm here. But I don't want to do anything else. I'd be crazy to let myself fall for that whole movie-star thing. Just because you're bored and you've been deprived of your diet of Hollywood women, doesn't mean you can use me as a substitute.' Her hand shaking, she rubbed her fingers over her forehead. 'I don't move in the same world as you. Quick meaningless sex just doesn't work for me.'

'Have you ever tried meaningless sex?' There was humour in those eyes. But there was also gentleness and it was the surprising gentleness that ripped at her self-control.

'No.'

'You should try everything once.'

'In that case you should try opening up and trusting. You might find a meaningful relationship really satisfying.'

Still holding her hands in his, he backed her against the rocks. 'Right now I know exactly what I'd find satisfying.'

Sandwiched between smooth rock and solid male muscle, Katie's willpower faltered. Her body throbbed and ached and excitement was a tight ball in the pit of her stomach. Sexual tension pulsed between them, the heat so intense that it was like flying into the sun. She stared up into his face, trying to read those eyes….

As he lowered his head towards her, she thought about the week they'd spent together. He'd told her nothing about himself. She knew no more now than she had when she'd worked in the theatre with him.

Katie planted a hand in the centre of his chest, feeling the steady beat of his heart under her fingers. 'Are you ever yourself?'

'What's that supposed to mean?'

'You're playing a role. Do you ever play yourself, Nathaniel?'

The change in him was almost imperceptible but it was there. Shimmering desire faded and his eyes were guarded. A tiny muscle flickered in his jaw and he watched her without speaking.

Then he released her in a smooth movement and stepped

away. The cynical, mocking look was back in his eyes. 'We would have been good together.'

Katie was glad she was leaning against the rock. Her knees were shaking so much she needed the support. Her hands ached to reach out for him, drag him back to her, lose herself in the heat of his mouth.

But she wanted it to be real, and this wasn't real.

They'd spent a week together, but she knew she hadn't spent a single moment with the real Nathaniel Wolfe.

His head throbbing from yet another sleepless night, Nathaniel flung snorkelling gear onto the deck while Ben and one of the other members of staff loaded food and equipment.

'Where are you going?' A soft, female voice came from behind him and he turned to see Katie standing on the jetty. Her feet were bare and her hands pushed into a pair of shorts. Even from a distance, he could feel her tension. Her cheeks were pale and there were dark shadows under her eyes.

Having spent most of the night wide awake in the hammock, it gave him some satisfaction to know that she wasn't sleeping any better than he was.

'*We* are going sailing. Given my misfortune of being trapped on this island with someone with your moral code, I need a distraction to take my mind off the total lack of meaningless sex.' *And a distraction to keep his mind off the new messages waiting on his phone.*

He picked up the final box and stowed it on board.

Katie didn't move. 'I think it would be best if I stayed here.'

'No, it wouldn't.' Before he could talk himself out of it, Nathaniel scooped her into his arms and deposited her onto the boat, keeping his eyes averted from her long, bare legs. 'This is one of the best dive sites in Brazil. You'll love it.'

'You're afraid to leave me here in case I tell someone where you are. What do you think I'm going to do, Nathaniel? Send up smoke signals? Even if I wanted to call someone, I can't. You locked up my phone.'

He wished he'd locked up his own. Those messages gnawed at him, acting like a block jammed in a door he was trying to slam shut.

'You don't need a phone.'

'You're afraid I'm going to tell someone about Annabelle or Carrie, but I swear I'm not going to mention their names to anyone. I don't even know who they are!'

It was possible to feel cold, he discovered, even when the sun was pounding down from high in the sky. 'I want you to forget you ever heard those names.'

'Fine, I'll forget I ever heard them. But once in a while it would be good for you to just trust someone. It must be incredibly lonely living a life where you think everyone is out to get you.' She pushed aside the snorkelling gear and sat down on the deck with a thump. 'I've never snorkelled. I'll probably drown.'

'You'll love it.'

'What if I inhale water?'

'I'll give you mouth-to-mouth.' Wishing he'd never allowed his mind to go in that direction, Nathaniel sprang onto the boat. 'Let's go.'

Under sail, the catamaran sped through the water, swift and smooth, responding well to the light winds. The water sparkled in the sunlight and shoals of colourful fish darted beneath them.

Katie stretched her legs out on the seat and tilted her face up to the sun.

Wondering whether he'd made a mistake bringing her, Nathaniel pushed the tiller away from him and sailed towards the wind, breathing deeply as the salty air touched his face. The position gave him a perfect view of her long slim legs, so he shifted slightly.

They sailed for several hours, past numerous deserted islands, and finally attached themselves to a mooring buoy so that they could snorkel around the reef.

Ignoring him, Katie stripped off her shorts and T-shirt to reveal a tiny red polka-dot bikini.

It was the first time she'd worn a bikini in front of him and he was starting to wish she'd stuck to drab, conceal-everything clothes. Sweat prickled the back of his neck.

Wishing he'd given her a wetsuit, he helped fit her mask and then they slid into the water.

'How deep is it here? On second thought, don't tell me. I don't want to know.' She held on to his arm tightly and looked around her. 'Is anything in this water going to want to eat me for lunch?'

Just him. Wondering if she'd even noticed he was aroused, Nathaniel showed her how to clear her mask and snorkel of water, trying to put some distance between them.

A shoal of parrot fish darted beneath them, playing hide and seek through fronds of tropical sea grass, and she gave a gasp of delight and dragged the snorkel out of her mouth. 'They're beautiful. Can we take a closer look?'

It took only moments for him to realise that she was an excellent swimmer, her kick smooth and graceful as she slid through the water with the elegance of a sea creature. Seriously distracted, Nathaniel decided that if he didn't concentrate he was going to drown.

Finally he gestured to the surface and they slid upwards through the sun-dappled water and emerged to hot sunshine.

Katie removed the snorkel from her mouth, laughing and gasping for air. 'That was fantastic!' Something over his shoulder caught her eye and she frowned. 'Nathaniel…'

He turned his head and saw that another boat had anchored only metres away from theirs. 'Relax. They don't know who we are.'

'You mean they have no idea I'm the famous costume designer? Thank goodness for that. If there's one thing I hate it's signing autographs in the water.' Giggling at her own joke, Katie watched the other boat. 'Looks like quite a party. Better keep your mask on.'

'Do you want to dive again?'

'What sort of a question is that? I want to do this for the rest of my life.' Without waiting for him, she ducked under the water and Nathaniel followed, surprised by how much he was enjoying himself.

They snorkelled for several hours, exploring different parts of the reef, careful not to touch or disturb any of the marine wildlife. Each time they surfaced she burst into a torrent of chat, telling him what she'd seen and asking question after question.

It was impossible not to make comparisons with the last woman he'd taken sailing who had spent her time lying on the deck topping up her suntan and protecting her hair. The mere suggestion that she might join him in the water had been greeted by unadulterated horror. Katie's hair hung over her shoulders in thick wet ropes but she didn't seem remotely self-conscious. Enraptured by what was going on beneath the surface of the water, she even seemed to have lost the awkwardness she felt around him.

When they finally climbed back onto the boat, her smile was as bright as the sun. 'That was the best thing I've ever done.' Her happiness was so infectious that Nathaniel found himself smiling back.

The dark mood that had gripped him since the night he'd walked off the stage had lifted. Realising that she was the one responsible for the lightness inside him, Nathaniel frowned.

He couldn't ever remember enjoying himself with a woman so much.

Dragging his eyes from that smile, he reminded himself

that the last thing he needed in his life was a woman who believed in happy endings.

He'd stopped believing in happy endings when he was nine years old.

Sipping her drink, Katie stared at the platinum-white sand of the distant beach. Her limbs ached and her skin stung from the combination of sun and sea water but she'd never felt happier. She'd even stopped sucking in her stomach.

Her gaze slid to Nathaniel, who was neatly looping a rope.

The chemistry between them had boosted her confidence.

And he wanted their relationship to go all the way. If he'd had his way they would have spent last night together.

He was Hollywood's hottest leading man, voted Sexiest Man by no fewer than ten leading women's magazines. Women screamed when he arrived at premieres.

And she'd said no.

Was she mad?

Raucous laughter from the nearby boat cut through her thoughts.

Katie glanced over her shoulder and saw two of the girls flirting with the men at the front of the boat. Missing the peace and wishing they hadn't chosen this part of the ocean for their sail, she was about to look away when movement caught her eye. Putting down her drink, she squinted into the sunshine. 'Nathaniel, that child is standing on the rail and she's not wearing a life jacket.'

As Nathaniel turned his head, the toddler leaned over a little too far and plopped helplessly into the deep water.

Katie shot to her feet in horror. She cupped her hands either side of her mouth and yelled, 'Hey!' at the top of her voice, but the distance and the music drowned out the sound and the adults on the boat were too busy partying to notice that the toddler had fallen in. 'Ben, turn the boat! Do something! We need to—'

There was a splash from beside her and droplets of water showered her as Nathaniel plunged into the sea in a smooth dive.

Still in shock, Katie stared as he powered through the water. It was an astonishing display of athleticism and if it hadn't been for the urgency of the moment she would have stopped and watched in awe. Instead she was frantic. 'Ben—'

'I know…' Ben was pulling up the anchor and Katie stood, agitated, helpless and wanting to help.

'What can I do?'

'Sit down and watch for Nathaniel. He's a strong swimmer. If anyone can get to the child, he can.' Ben started the engine and turned the boat. 'I daren't get too close because of the propeller. Can you see him?'

'No. He's diving down exactly where the toddler fell in, but it's so deep, Ben.' Katie's palms were slippery on the side of the boat. Panic weakened her limbs. 'I'm going in too. I might be able to help.'

Ben didn't try to stop her and Katie plunged into the water after Nathaniel.

He still hadn't surfaced and it seemed impossible to her that he could have held his breath for all that time.

Under the water Katie realised that she should have grabbed the mask so that she could see more clearly. She kicked her legs and dived as deep as she could but her lungs were already bursting for air and she could see nothing. The mysterious underwater world that had captivated them earlier had now formed a deadly trap.

Heart pounding, her chest aching, she was about to surface when she saw Nathaniel a few metres away, manoeuvring something wedged under a large boulder. She saw a white arm and a leg and realised with a flash of panic that the child had somehow become wedged under the rock. The burning in her chest was so intense that she had no choice but to surface and breathe. How Nathaniel could have stayed under for so long, she had no idea.

The group on the nearby boat still hadn't noticed the absence of the toddler, their music and laughter drowning out everything around them.

Nathaniel surfaced next to her and dragged in a lungful of air. His dark hair was plastered to his head, his sodden lashes framing eyes blazing with determination. Almost immediately he dived under the water again.

A commotion from the other boat told her that the toddler's absence had finally been discovered and there was a pounding of feet and shrieks as they realised what had happened. They hung over the side, yelling the little girl's name and Katie felt hot tears scald her eyes, horrified by how quickly paradise had turned to hell.

She kept watching, hoping.

And then Nathaniel finally surfaced, the limp toddler in his arms.

'Ben—' The strain was visible as he swept his hand over his face to clear the water. 'Take her. Get her on a flat surface.'

Ben reached down and took the child in his large hands, laying her on the floor of the boat, and Nathaniel immediately put his hands on the side of the boat and levered himself out of the water in a smooth, fluid motion.

Envying his athletic ability, Katie struggled back into the boat. Nathaniel was performing mouth-to-mouth and chest compressions with grim focus. He seemed oblivious to the screams and sobs coming from the occupants of the other boat. It was as if this was one challenge he was determined not to lose. 'Come on, baby girl—' he turned his head to listen to her chest '—breathe for me, sweetheart. Breathe…'

Moved by the tenderness in his voice, Katie dropped to her knees next to him. 'Nathaniel—'

The toddler coughed and vomited weakly and Nathaniel

immediately rolled her on her side into the recovery position, his hands gentle and confident.

'That's a good girl. You'll be all right, now. You're going to be fine….'

Weak with relief, Katie looked at him expecting to see similar emotion reflected in his face but instead saw a man who was clearly traumatised.

Underneath the bronzed good looks, his face was ashen.

Realising just how much the rescue must have taken out of him, she put her hand on his arm.

'You did it,' she croaked, wondering if he realised what he'd achieved. 'Nathaniel, you saved her. You were so brave. And determined. If it hadn't been for you—' Unashamed to discover that she was crying, Katie was about to say something else when the little girl wriggled weakly onto all fours, still choking and coughing.

'Want Mummy…'

Nathaniel rubbed the child's back gently, his strong hands soothing as he comforted the toddler. 'You're going to be fine, angel.' But there were dark shadows in his eyes that Katie didn't understand.

Shouldn't he be celebrating?

There were shouts from the water and lots of splashing as two of the adults from the other boat swam the short distance towards Nathaniel's boat. '*Nina?* Is she alive?'

In a single decisive movement, Nathaniel rose and vanished into the saloon.

By the time the couple boarded the boat there was no sign of him.

'Oh, thank God, thank God…' The couple scooped up the toddler and thanked Ben profusely.

He accepted their thanks calmly, suggested they take the child to be checked by the doctor who worked on the island and pointed out that the little girl should have been wearing a life jacket.

Katie wanted to yell that they were thanking the wrong person but she understood that Nathaniel hadn't wanted to be recognised and the couple were too relieved to have their child safe to show too much interest in the identity of the rescuer.

She sat, numb, as Ben skilfully moved the two boats alongside so that the rapidly recovering toddler could be transferred with the minimum of fuss.

Now that it was over, Katie found that she was shaking and shivering like a leaf in a storm. She grabbed a dry towel from the deck and wrapped it around herself but the shivering wouldn't stop. The sun shone high overhead, and yet she felt cold. *Really cold.*

If she felt like this, how was Nathaniel feeling?

Nathaniel leaned over the toilet, retching violently. The horror of it gripped him like a physical force. He'd taken refuge in the cabin, not because of the risk of being recognised, but because he'd been afraid he was going to humiliate himself right there in the middle of the boat.

Water. A drowning child. Sick panic.

Wasn't it ever going to go away?

Lifting his head, he looked in the mirror. Staring back at him was a face so deathly pale he would have made a corpse look healthy. And as for his eyes—he gave a humourless laugh—if the eyes were windows to the soul, then he was definitely in trouble.

Not wanting to see what was through those windows, he closed his eyes, but immediately saw the child flailing, helpless in the water. Drowning, her lungs screaming for air as she sank in her watery grave.

Nathaniel turned on the taps and tried to splash his face but his hands were shaking so badly most of the water landed on the floor. His stomach churned like the ocean in a storm and his body felt shaky and weak.

Alpha Man? He gave a bitter laugh at the evidence of his own weakness.

Under his feet, he felt the shift of the deck and realised the boat was moving.

Ben, he thought gratefully. Thank goodness for Ben.

He needed to get the hell off the water.

CHAPTER SIX

KATIE lay in the hammock, her book unopened. Beneath her, a kaleidoscope of sea life darted through clear, turquoise water but her brain was too preoccupied to enjoy her idyllic surroundings.

The moment the boat had approached the island, Nathaniel had jumped into the sea and waded the last few metres to the shore without glance or conversation.

Maybe it was just delayed reaction. Maybe he needed time to himself.

If Nathaniel wanted to be alone, then there was no way she was going to force herself on him. In his position she would have been talking it through, but he was different, wasn't he?

Katie opened her book and stared at the first page. After she'd read the same line five times, she gave up and stared at the horizon. Images of Nathaniel diving into the water played across her brain. It wasn't the bold rescue that stayed with her, although that in itself had been impressive. What really affected her was the look on his face. The fierce determination in his eyes was something she'd never forget.

Remembering the mother's frenzied, hysterical relief as she'd held her child, Katie shivered.

Without Nathaniel it would have been so different.

Alpha Man.

Even she could see that with the Sapphire Award ceremony only a week away it would have been a perfect publicity opportunity. And yet he hadn't taken it. He'd made sure the child was safe and then he'd left the scene quickly before anyone had a chance to recognise him. It didn't make sense.

None of it made sense.

Katie gave up on the book and swung her legs out of the hammock. She'd just check on him, she told herself, and then she'd give him space.

Barefoot, she walked along the terrace that circled the villa, breathing in the heavy scent of tropical plants. As she approached the terrace of the master bedroom she paused, still worried about intruding. It wasn't as if they had a relationship. They were castaways, thrown here together by accident. They weren't friends. They weren't lovers.

Lovers.

She shivered at the word, thinking of that first night when they'd come so close. And last night on the beach—

Impatient with herself, Katie breathed deeply and walked onto the deck. She was doing what any human being would do in the circumstances. Offering comfort.

She found him sprawled on the swing seat, staring out across the sea as the sun went down.

'Nathaniel? You didn't eat dinner. Do you want Ben to bring you something?'

'No. I want to be on my own.' Both words and tone were a warning to back off.

Katie ignored the warning and sat down next to him. The decision earned her a cautionary look.

'I never saw you as a risk taker.'

'Maybe you don't know me as well as you think.'

And she didn't know him, did she? She knew nothing about him. He let the world see the actor, never the man. 'You were amazing today. You know how to play the hero in real life as well as in the movies.' It still shocked her to think how quickly the day had changed. How death had lurked in those calm, clear waters.

'I feel pretty shaken up, so goodness knows how you're feeling.' She decided to take a risk and plunged. 'Talk to me, Nathaniel. Tell me why you're sitting here on your own, pushing me away.' *Show yourself to me. Don't hide....*

The silence was thick and heavy. 'Talking isn't going to change the fact that she almost drowned.'

'But she didn't drown. You saved her. She's lucky you're such a good swimmer who loves the water so much.'

'I hate the water.' The confession was wrenched violently from somewhere deep inside him. 'The reason I'm a good swimmer is because I *hate* the water.' He turned his head and she saw such intense suffering that she sat still, immobilised by the agony reflected in those perfect features.

It was like a veil falling down. She'd wanted him to show himself, but the reality was almost too painful to watch. In his face, she saw nothing but dark, sinister shadows. They lurked in the depths of his eyes, settled around the line of his mouth and haunted the hard angle of his jaw. Emotion. Raw and brutally real. The actor had vanished and she was looking at the man.

Shocked into silence, as far out of her depth as the helpless child in the water, Katie felt a desperate need to ease his anguish in whatever way she could. She moved her hand towards his and then withdrew it, afraid of doing anything that might be a catalyst for his withdrawal. 'Do you want to tell me why?'

His laugh was harsh. 'Do you want to hear it?'

'Yes.' She held her breath, feeling the fragility of the moment and afraid to damage it with clumsy words. 'Yes, I do.'

'Are you sure? You and I don't live in the same world. You live in Katie-land.'

'Stop saying that.'

'Why? It's true.' It was the low, warning growl of a wounded animal. 'You believe that people are basically good and that happy endings come to those who wait. You believe in love.' He spoke the word with cynical emphasis that said everything there was to be said about his own belief system.

This time she did take his hand and held tightly, refusing to let him pull away. 'We're talking about you, not me. Tell me why you hate the water.'

The silence stretched for so long she started to think that he was never going to talk.

And then he spoke. 'There was a lake—' his voice was hoarse '—in the grounds of our house. I grew up in this huge, soulless stately home. Wolfe Manor. A privileged upbringing, or so everyone always told me. It was big. Big enough to play hide and seek and never get found, which was useful because hiding was part of how I lived.'

'Who were you hiding from, Nathaniel?'

He stared into the darkness, his eyes focused on nothing. 'The lake was huge. No matter how blue the sky, the water was always dark. Just below the surface you could see the weeds, floating like tentacles ready to grab an ankle. None of us knew how deep it was, but we did know that one of our ancestors had drowned there.'

Katie shivered, although whether it was the words or the tone, she didn't know. 'It sounds like a pretty menacing place.'

'When we were very young we used to believe that a monster lurked in the middle.'

Without thinking, she lifted her hand and smoothed her fingers over his face. Her fingertips registered the roughness of stubble and the perfect symmetry of his jaw. Those smouldering good looks belonged to the man. There was no trace of the boy in his face, but it was surprisingly easy to imagine how he might have been back then, a child, standing by that lake, fascinated and horrified in equal measure, terrified of the monster.

'What happened?' She asked the question in the absolute certainty that something had. 'Nathaniel?'

His blue eyes fixed on hers with a fierce intensity, revealing indecision and a deeply inbred reluctance to share with anyone.

After a moment he stood abruptly and paced to the front of the terrace. His hands curled over the railing, his knuckles white with the force of his grip.

'It was late evening. Dark. I'd been doing something I shouldn't—as usual. Messing about. My father picked me up and threw me in that lake.' His voice shook with repressed emotion. 'I don't know whether it was the look on his face just before he hurled me in or the words he spoke, but the shock froze all my reactions. I didn't even struggle. When I hit the water I thought, *This is it, I'm going to drown.* I remember wondering how long it would take and whether it was going to hurt. I remember struggling below the surface, trying to get my legs free of the weeds, watching his back as he walked away, thinking, *He'll come back and save me in a minute.* He didn't.' He kept his back to her, his voice strangely flat as he recounted an incident so sickening that for once Katie found herself without words as she struggled to absorb the full implications of that driven confession.

'No.' Her voice trembled with uncertainty. She thought about her own father, of the games they'd played where he'd tumbled her upside down and tossed her in the air. 'It must have been a joke that went wrong. He must have been playing a game.'

'He wasn't playing. Afterwards I tried to rationalise it to myself. I'd been messing around instead of raking the leaves. I'd had it coming to me. I was so young I didn't really understand.' He recited the options in a flat tone. 'I thought it was me. My fault. I thought if I did the right thing, he'd love me.

It isn't easy for a child to absorb the fact that isn't ever going to happen.'

He'd wanted his daddy's approval, the way all little boys did.

He'd wanted love. Wasn't that the minimum any child should expect from a parent?

Katie felt the numbness spread through her body. She'd never felt so inadequate, not even when her father had died and the whole ghastly mess he'd left had come to light. She wanted to say exactly the right thing but how could you say anything right about something so wrong?

Nathaniel turned his head to look at her. His eyes were hard and his mouth slanted into a cynical smile. 'Poor Katie. Now I've destroyed your essential belief that all human beings are good and that life always ends in a happy ever after.'

She roused herself. 'I don't think that. I don't think that all human beings are good, but…' She drew breath, struggling to imagine how it must feel to have a father that brutal. 'What about your mother?'

'Ah, my mother…' His expression altered. 'Well, the one thing you need to know about my mother was that she was in love with my father. She only ever wanted one thing and that was for him to love her back. He didn't, of course. My father didn't love anyone.' His tone was derisive and contemptuous, layered with bitterness and years of pain and rejection. 'He was the wrong guy for someone as sensitive and fragile as my mother. It was like placing Venetian glass under a sledgehammer. He shattered her. She…left.'

Katie winced at the image he drew. 'So you were left alone with your father?' *The man he'd described was a monster.*

'*Not* on my own. Some aristocratic English families collect Renaissance art or Louis XV furniture. My father collected women. And those women had children. Children my father was never interested in.'

'He didn't want children?'

'My father was interested only in himself.'

Katie stood and the swing creaked. Her feet silent on the deck, she took two steps and placed her hands on his shoulders. Her fingers encountered knots of tension under hard solid muscle. 'Who rescued you from the lake that day? How did you survive?'

'My half-brother Jacob. He was nine years older than me and it wasn't the first time he'd fished me out of the lake.' Something flickered in his eyes. 'His role in the family was to clear up my father's mess. He hauled me choking out of the water, pumped the water out of my lungs and kept me out of the monster's way until he'd drunk enough to forget I even existed.'

'Nathaniel—'

'It's all right. You don't have to try and find the right thing to say. In this case, there really isn't anything. Even someone with your sweet, sunny nature can't put a positive spin on a father like mine, although for years I tried to do just that.'

'Is he still alive?'

'No. He died when I was nine years old.' His voice was savage. 'You think you've heard the worst? Ask me how my father died, Katie. Ask me that question.'

The air around them felt thick and heavy. 'How did he die?'

'We were all home from boarding school for the holidays. My sister had taken advantage of his absence to sneak out of the house to a party in the village. She wasn't even fourteen, but she was already stunning and that night she decided to flaunt it. Lipstick, miniskirt—' He broke off, his face several shades paler than normal. 'It would have been fine, except that he came back early.'

'Your father?'

'He'd seen her flirting in the village and when he arrived home he took a whip to her.'

Katie flinched, her imagination making it all too easy to imagine the cruel bite of the whip. 'He beat her?'

'His intention was to make sure no boy would ever look at her again, but he was drunk and out of control and he beat her so brutally that he would have killed her if Jacob hadn't stopped him. And the whole time I stood there shaking and yelling, "Stop it! Stop it!"' He stared down at his shaking hands. 'That night I learned how it felt to be helpless. Powerless.'

Katie's face was soaked with tears. 'Nathaniel, you were a *child*. What could you possibly have done?'

'We should have fought him. But we shouted at him, Sebastian and I,' Nathaniel said hoarsely. 'And just when I thought it was all over, that he was going to kill her with us watching, Jacob walked through the door.'

'He stopped him?'

'He killed him.' Nathaniel turned his head to look at her. His eyes were empty. Tired. 'It was an accident—he was so drunk that he fell and his head cracked against the stairs and then…' His brow furrowed. 'There was so much blood. My father's blood, Annabelle's blood, her beautiful face a torn mess. Jacob was frozen with shock. And my father was dead.'

Annabelle?

Annabelle was his sister?

Digesting that fact, Katie stood still, hopelessly inadequate in the face of so much pain. 'I don't know what to say. I'm so sorry.'

'I wasn't.' He turned and locked his hand in the front of her shirt and hauled her against him, his eyes the deep, menacing colour of a sea in a storm. 'I wasn't sorry, Katie. I stood there thinking, *Now it will stop*. But I wasn't sorry.' His voice was thickened with a vile mess of emotion, from guilt to bitter anger. 'So now you know. Now you know who I really am. Your world and my world don't even overlap.' He released her so suddenly she staggered. The intensity of emotion pulsed from him like a living force and suddenly she realised just how much he kept locked inside, hidden away from the world.

'Do you feel guilty for not being sorry? Is that what's wrong? You were just a child, Nathaniel.' She slid her arms around his waist but he stood rigid and unresponsive.

'He was my father, and I hated him. That makes me the monster.'

'It makes you human.' Her throat thickened by tears, Katie rubbed her hands over the tense muscles of his back and then slid her arms around the strong column of his neck. 'You're not a monster, Nathaniel. You were a little boy who wanted, and deserved, to be loved by his father.'

'At the time I assumed it was shock.' It was as if he was talking to himself. 'I assumed I'd wake up one day and feel sorry that it had happened. I'm still waiting to feel sorry.'

She pressed her lips to his chest, as if her touch could heal his agony. 'You have no reason to feel guilty.'

'I didn't protect my sister.'

'You were a child!'

His beautiful mouth twisted into a cynical smile. 'We weren't allowed to be children.'

They stood for a moment in silence and then she lifted her head. 'What happened to Jacob?'

'There were expensive lawyers in sharp suits. They sorted it.'

So few words to describe such a hideous trauma.

'But that didn't make it go away, did it? You all had to live with that. Who took care of you?'

'To begin with, Jacob. Then one day he just took off.' In the dim light, his eyes shone a deep, glittering blue. 'That was the day I really thought Annabelle might die. I guess she saw him as the one stable person in our very unstable family. She loved him *so* much.' He gave a crooked smile. '*Big* mistake.

If you don't care, you can't get hurt. Annabelle cared, and she got herself badly hurt.'

And not just Annabelle.

If you don't care, you can't get hurt.

That was why he avoided relationships. Not because he didn't believe in love, but because he was afraid of love. He associated love with carnage, both emotional and physical.

'You must have felt so lost and vulnerable, losing your father and then Jacob.' Katie hesitated. 'When you walked off the stage that night, you kept saying, "I have to warn Annabelle." What were you warning her about, Nathaniel? What really happened on opening night?'

'Jacob was in the audience.'

'And you haven't seen him for a while?'

There was a long silence. 'I last saw Jacob twenty years ago.'

'Twenty years!' Katie couldn't hide her shock. 'You haven't seen him since he walked out?'

'We're not what you'd call a close family. As reunions went, this one wasn't exactly successful.'

Katie found it difficult to absorb. 'No wonder you reacted the way you did—no wonder you walked out.'

'I kept thinking about Annabelle. How his sudden reappearance would affect her. I just wanted to warn her he was back.'

So he hadn't been involved in some complex love triangle. When he'd said, 'He's here,' he'd been referring to his half-brother Jacob. And Annabelle was his sister.

When he'd walked off the stage, he'd been intent on protecting the sister he believed he'd failed all those years ago.

Her heart ached for the lonely little boy, hurt and abandoned by those who should have loved him.

The soft sound of the sea licked at the air and the smell of tropical flowers tinged the night with sweetness.

The stark contrast between the idyllic surroundings and his brutal, loveless childhood was acute.

His mother had left. His father had beaten him. He had little or no contact with his family. No wonder he was hard and cynical when she talked about family. She winced, remembering all the things she'd said. Katie-land. She'd been insensitive. If she'd known…

'Have you spoken to Annabelle?'

'We exchanged a text.'

'A text? That's it? No conversation?'

'This is the Wolfe family.' His tone mocking, he reached out and picked a brightly coloured hibiscus from the profusion of flowers that crowded the terrace. 'If our background taught us one thing, it was how to survive alone. A text is a lot for Annabelle.'

'But you love your sister.' She said it as fact, not as a question. 'And Jacob—'

'When I saw him in the front row of the theatre I felt nothing but uncontrollable rage, but those feelings were all mixed up with seeing my father beating Annabelle that night.' Nathaniel stared at the flower in his hands. 'I left without speaking to him. And I still don't want to speak to him. It's in the past. I don't want to go back there.'

Instinctively she knew who was making those calls he ignored. 'The two of you must talk.'

'Talk.' His tone mocking, he turned to her and slid the scarlet flower into her hair. 'Katie's answer to all life's problems.'

Katie blocked out the sensuous stroke of his hands in her hair. 'If you've never talked about that night, then surely it's time you did.'

'Why?' His eyes were bleak and empty. 'We can't change what happened. We can't change who we've become. It isn't possible.'

'But it is possible to change the future. And the present.

And the way you feel about the past. You didn't let Annabelle down—you wanted to help her.' She tried not to feel disappointed as his hands dropped to his sides. 'I'm glad you told me.'

'Why? Because now you have a juicy story to tell the press?'

'You know I wouldn't do that.' She reminded herself that he was raw and hurting.

'Go to bed, Katie. We should never have started this conversation.' He turned away from her, his broad shoulders forming yet another barrier between himself and the world.

Braced for rejection, she placed her hand on his back. The heat of his skin burned through his shirt and she frowned.

'You're burning up.'

He turned, his eyes glittering dangerously—a cold, fierce blue loaded with warning. 'I don't want your sympathy. Go to bed.'

'Why? So that you can wallow and feel bad in private? I'm not leaving you, Nathaniel. You've tried dealing with this on your own. Now try the other alternative. I'm not walking away.'

'Why? What is it that you want?'

She stood, poised and breathless as a diver on the highest board about to plunge. 'I want you.' She'd never wanted anything so much. She wanted it more than she wanted to protect herself. Because of that, the words were remarkably easy to say. 'I want you.'

'I've been offering you that all week.' He kept his hands by his sides. 'You rejected it.'

'You offered me Nathaniel Wolfe, the actor. I'm not interested in him. I want the man. I want to know it's real.'

'You don't want the man and you can't handle real.'

Katie caught his arm before he could turn away again. 'Don't tell me what I want. Don't tell me what I can handle.'

'Real isn't always pretty, Katie. Most people prefer their

reality tempered with a little gloss. That's why they go to the movies. They don't want real.'

'I do. I'm not afraid of that. I'm more afraid when you're acting because then I can't trust anything you say or do. Don't hide from me, Nathaniel.' Her fingers threaded through his and she felt his hesitation. And that hesitation punctured her confidence. Insecurity spread in widening ripples through her body. There was assertive and then there was pushy. He wasn't just 'a man,' was he? He was Nathaniel Wolfe, A-list movie star and sex god. What if he didn't really want her? What if the flirtation had just been his way of relieving boredom?

When he still didn't touch her, Katie took a step backwards, wishing she could vanish.

The embarrassment was hideous.

'Right.' She conjured up brightness to cover the oceans of humiliation. 'Well, obviously you can't always have what you want, so I'll just—' The words were crushed under his mouth as he hauled her against him, his hands rough and his body hard.

'Is this real enough for you?' He spoke the words against her lips and his eyes blazed hot into hers. When she didn't answer, he took her mouth, his kiss rough and demanding. His movements were jerky and unsynchronised and yet the desperation in his touch was more erotic than any of the smooth, choreographed movements of their previous encounters. The hands that dug into her hair shook slightly, and when he yanked at her dress he fumbled in his desperation to strip her naked.

'How does this—?' Impatient, he tore it from neck to hem and she gasped, excited and nervous at the same time.

'Nathaniel—'

'I want you.' His mouth was at her throat. Her head tipped back and her nerves exploded with heat. 'I want you so badly….' His hands were rough as he scooped her up and deposited her on the bed but she revelled in the desperation she sensed in him.

For once, he wasn't in control.

It wasn't about camera angles or movements—it was about a primitive, elemental driving force that transcended everything. It was just about the two of them. And an explosive physical attraction like nothing she'd ever felt before. It felt real. It felt right.

His hands were in her hair, his hungry mouth awaking feelings so intense that she shook with the force of it. She ripped at his shirt and he helped her, his mouth still on hers as he tore it off so that she could touch him. And then he was crushing her against the bed. His fingers skimmed her body, exploring her intimately until fire licked through her veins and heated her skin. And she touched him too, fascinated by the dip and swell of muscle, by the contrast of sleek and rough.

Sounds mingled in the night air. The swish of the sea on the beach, a soft sigh from low in her throat as his touch grew more intimate. The pleasure rose to burning excitement, every part of her trembling and quivering as she writhed in a fever of anticipation.

And then he was above her and she sobbed in desperation as she felt the hard heat of him against her. With a single thrust he filled her and she gave a sharp cry of shock because it was so much more than she'd anticipated. Holding herself tense, she was aware of his harsh breathing, of the tension in his powerful frame as he forced himself to hold still.

'Katie—'

'I—I'm OK…it's OK.' But she was afraid to breathe, afraid she couldn't accommodate the size of him.

With a soft curse, he started to withdraw but she closed her hands over his hips. 'Don't stop. I don't want you to stop….'

His head dropped to her shoulder and he paused for a moment, buried deep, his breathing unsteady. Then he lifted his head and his eyes burned into hers.

'Look at me.'

And she did.

Holding her gaze, he lowered his head and kissed her gently, seducing her mouth with slow, practised kisses until her whole body was shivering.

'Relax, sweetheart…' He murmured the words against her lips, holding himself still as her body melted around him, until she was moaning and quivering. Then he started to move, slowly at first, infinitely gentle as he taught her what her body could do.

It was overwhelming. Like nothing she'd ever experienced or imagined.

'Nathaniel—' Her voice broke and he slid his hand under her hips and drew her against him, controlling her pleasure.

The excitement was fierce and hot, clawing at her as he increased the rhythm, and she met each driving thrust with wild abandon. It was wild and crazy and the climax hit like a violent storm. As it crashed down on them, Katie clung to his slick shoulders, shattered by the violence of the emotion that swamped both of them.

'It was your first time.' Nathaniel lay on his back, his forearm over his forehead, not sure whether he was supposed to feel guilty or smug. The truth was he didn't recognise any of the feelings inside him. He didn't know whether what they'd just shared was a mistake or a miracle.

Damn.

She snuggled against him. 'So?'

'If I'd known, I would have stopped.' *Or would he?* Nathaniel shifted uncomfortably, disturbed by how out of control he'd been. When had he ever felt like that before? Flirtation, dinner, jewellery, sex—it was a well-rehearsed sequence that required no thought, effort or emotional engagement.

What he'd shared with Katie was different.

He'd shared something with her he'd never shared with another person.

Himself.

The knowledge sat in a tight, uncomfortable knot in his stomach. Something close to panic gripped him. It wasn't just the fear of what she might do with the information that bothered him, it was the fact that he'd told her at all.

Why had he told her? He never talked about his family. He went to extraordinary lengths to conceal his past. He'd reinvented himself as someone different.

But rescuing the toddler had brought it all rushing back. He'd been a child again, plunged into the dark, oily waters of the lake. Unfortunately Katie's internal radar for anyone in distress was alarmingly sophisticated.

And long range, he thought grimly, remembering how she'd tracked him down.

Unlike other women who were only interested in the glitz and glamour of life, Katie wanted reality.

And he'd given her a hefty dose.

Realising that she was unusually silent, he turned his head to look at her and discovered she'd fallen asleep, her hair a wild tumble around her shoulders, a smile on that gorgeous mouth. A strand of hair had curled itself around his arm and he lifted his hand and touched it, feeling the silken softness coil around his fingers.

She was the most optimistic person he'd ever met.

Apparently even the ugly truth of his childhood hadn't been enough to send her running.

She'd had sex with him because she believed she'd finally seen the 'real' Nathaniel.

And that, he reflected bitterly, had been his biggest mistake in this whole crazy mess, because he had no wish to be the real Nathaniel. He'd left the real Nathaniel behind decades ago and that was the way he wanted it to stay.

CHAPTER SEVEN

KATIE woke with the sun on her face. A breeze whispered through the open doors and she could hear the soft lap of water against the edge of the pool.

Aching, happy, she opened her eyes and the first thing she saw was the empty space next to her.

Nathaniel had gone.

A shadow veiled her happiness but she pushed it aside. It was late, wasn't it? Of course he was already up.

He'd let her sleep late.

Refusing to allow herself to overanalyse what could simply be a thoughtful gesture, she took a quick shower and slid into her favourite canary-yellow sundress. Spotting the tropical flower he'd given her the night before, she slid it into her hair. The scent of it brought everything rushing back and her whole body was suffused with a warm glow. She felt special. Not because of the sex, although that had been incredible—no, the reason she felt special was because he'd confided in her. He'd trusted her with his darkest, deepest secrets—something she suspected he hadn't shared with anyone before.

As she walked out onto the terrace, she told herself it was ridiculous to feel nervous after the intimacies they'd shared the night before.

Nathaniel was talking on the phone. His hair gleamed in the sunlight and his striking blue eyes were fixed on a point in the distance. Distracted by his flawless features and sensual mouth, Katie's confidence faltered.

He looked like a superstar.

For a brief, crazy moment she wondered whether she'd imagined the whole thing.

Trying to forget that he was a movie star, she reminded herself that they'd just spent the most incredible night together. They'd connected, not just physically but emotionally. *He'd trusted her.*

Waiting for him to finish on the phone, she walked forward, wishing she possessed his acting skills. 'You should have woken me. I didn't mean to sleep this late.'

'I had some calls to make. It appears my agent has earned his keep. The situation in London has been smoothed over.' Reserved and distant, he gestured to the empty chair. 'Coffee?'

Disappointment thudded into her gut like a fist. *That was it?* That was what the night had meant to him? Only a few minutes ago she'd woken up feeling as though life couldn't get any better. The gulf between expectation and reality was shocking.

'Coffee would be great, thanks.' Formal. Polite. Two people forced to live together on the island—not two people who had rolled naked and wild, tangling sheets between their heated bodies.

Had it really meant nothing?

'Help yourself to pancakes and fresh fruit. We have an hour until the helicopter arrives.'

'Helicopter?' Katie put the cup down without taking a sip. 'We're leaving?' She was disturbed by just how much that bothered her. A week ago she hadn't even wanted to come here, and now—

'Just the island. We're going to spend some time in Rio.' Still not looking at her, he scrolled through his emails as if it were the beginning of a normal working day while Katie stared sickly at the food on the table. Embarrassment washed over her. How long had he watched her while she slept? Had he seen her in daylight and regretted what they'd shared? Frustration and anger mingled with the pain. But the anger was mostly directed at herself. Had she really been naïve enough to think she'd interest a man like him?

'Why are we going to Rio?'

'I've had enough of being trapped on an island. There's only so much solitude I can take.' His casual dismissal fed her insecurities and Katie stood quickly, the chair scraping the floor. Her eyes stung. The rejection sat like a solid lump in the pit of her stomach.

'Thanks a lot. So the part you're playing this morning is obviously "utter bastard."'

His eyes narrowed warily. 'What are you talking about?'

'If you'd been playing "nice guy" you might have thought that what we shared last night was at least deserving of a morning-after smile. You're making me feel horrid about myself.'

His eyes shone with incredulity. 'How?'

'Do you really have to ask? Are you really that insensitive?' Katie wrapped her arms around herself, wishing she'd taken the time to put on make-up and do her hair before facing him. No woman with any sense would choose the 'natural' look around Nathaniel Wolfe. 'We spent the night together and now you're doing everything you can to get away from me.' She felt really foolish for believing even for a moment that they'd shared something special. 'I understand that what happened yesterday was awful for you. I understand it brought everything back and maybe what we did was heat-of-the-moment stuff. If you regret last night, just say so. But don't act like nothing happened.'

'Sit down, Katie.'

'Why? So that you can make me feel even more insignificant than you have already? I don't think so. You're an incredible actor, Nathaniel, but I'm not interested in the actor and you don't want to be the man.' Totally squashed, utterly humiliated, she stalked off the terrace, throwing words over her shoulder. 'Go to Rio. Go to hell. I really don't care. Just don't follow me.'

What the hell did she want from him?

His hand shaking, Nathaniel finished his coffee and ordered another one. It had taken all his willpower to leave the bed before she woke. In the end, what had driven him had been the fact that he'd wanted to stay there, wrapped around Katie for ever. And the terror had acted as a jet-propelled engine.

For ever?

He wiped the sweat from his brow with his forearm. Those were words he just didn't use.

Utterly spooked by his feelings, he hadn't even trusted himself to look at her when she'd walked onto the terrace. He'd hoped for baggy brown clothes but she'd chosen bright yellow, the colour of sunshine and happiness.

Not that it had taken him long to kill that happiness, he thought bitterly.

Right now she was probably changing back into brown.

Ben brought the coffee to the table, his usually friendly smile absent. 'I just saw Miss Katie running towards the beach.' He thumped the pot down on the table and some of it sloshed over the side. 'Looked like she was crying.'

Nathaniel looked at the puddle of spilled coffee. 'She just needs space.'

'Not all folks need space when they're upset. Miss Katie is the sort who would prefer someone to talk to.'

Meeting Ben's accusatory look, Nathaniel felt fingers of ice trail down his spine. She wanted to talk about feelings and there was no way he wanted to even think about his feelings, let alone talk about them.

'You've known her five minutes—'

'Some people you get to know in five minutes because they're open and friendly. Others…' Ben's gaze didn't shift. 'Others keep themselves locked away.'

Locked away sounded good to him. 'Everyone is different.'

'She's trying to help you. In all my years I never met a kinder, warmer person than Miss Katie.'

'I don't need anyone's help.'

'Depends where you're standing.' Ben picked up Katie's abandoned cup. 'I'll clear up this mess.' The message was clear. Nathaniel was supposed to clear up the other mess. The one he'd made.

Cursing himself for allowing his guard to drop, Nathaniel abandoned the coffee and strode along the little path that wound through the tropical gardens down to the beach.

One conversation, he promised himself. *One.*

He found her on the perfect curve of soft sand that was Turtle Cove, her yellow sundress blending with the sand, her dark hair tumbling down her back.

Remembering the way she'd looked when she'd first arrived on the island, Nathaniel felt something twist inside him. She'd lost her dull, brown feathers and now she reminded him of an exotic bird. And last night—

'Katie…'

She didn't turn but her shoulders grew a little stiffer. 'I want to be by myself.'

Nathaniel would have loved to have taken that claim at face value but Ben's voice was still ringing in his ears, and on top of that his conscience, which rarely even got out of bed in the morning, was now working overtime.

'Look—' his tone was impatient '—you have to understand that this isn't easy for me. I don't do relationships, not the sort you dream about anyway. I have short term, mutually convenient affairs with women who don't want any more connection than I do. You're different. For God's sake, Katie—' he dragged his hand through his hair '—you'd never even been with a man before.'

'I don't want to talk about this.'

He felt a flash of exasperation. 'Why not? You want to talk about everything else. I know you're upset because I didn't stay in bed this morning—'

'I'm upset because last night I saw the real Nathaniel, and now you've turned back into the movie star. I don't know you like this.'

And that was the idea, wasn't it?

Staring at the back of her head, Nathaniel felt as though there was a battle going on in his brain. 'I'm not good at being the "real Nathaniel,"' he ground out. 'I'm not good at letting people know me.'

'You prefer to hide behind the actor.'

'Yes.' The admission was easier than he'd thought it would be. 'It's what I've always done.'

She turned then and he saw the wetness on her cheeks. Guilt lanced through him, sharp as a blade. Usually when women used tears they left him unaffected. Seeing Katie's reddened eyes made his insides clench with panic.

'Don't cry,' he breathed. 'Don't do that….'

'Answer me something honestly.' Her voice was croaky. 'Is it Carrie? I know you said you weren't having an affair with her, but—'

'It isn't Carrie.' Just saying the name made him want to turn and run, but he fought it. He knew he ought to tell her the truth about Carrie, but he'd carried the secret for too long to part with it easily. 'It's nothing to do with Carrie. It's me. This is who I am.'

She was silent and that silence was another tug on his conscience. Nathaniel scanned her face. 'Say something. Yell at me. Tell me what I should be feeling, doing…' He looked at her desperately. 'It's not like you to be silent.'

'You don't like it when I talk.'

'I do.' It came as a surprise to realise it was true. 'Yesterday when we were on that boat, and you were saying everything that came into your head—'

'I drove you nuts.'

'No, I enjoyed it. A lot. I really like the way you say what you're thinking.'

'You never say what you're thinking.' Her gaze was steady. 'And I find it impossible to tell what's real. With you, it's all too easy to get it wrong because you're so good at what you do.'

He tried to find a way to tell her that the whole idea of 'real' scared the hell out of him. 'Last night was real, Katie.'

'No, it wasn't. We had sex. I played the part of a gullible female and you played the part of the macho, virile caveman.'

'Are you saying I hurt you?' It was something that had worried him and he saw her cheeks redden.

'You didn't hurt me. Not last night.'

He'd hurt her this morning, with careless words and his own inability to let his guard down. Burying those thoughts, Nathaniel pulled her to her feet. When she tried to resist him he tightened his hold and found her mouth with his.

'Go away.' She turned her head. 'You regret last night.'

'I don't regret last night. At least not the part where you were naked and uninhibited. That bit was incredible. *You* were incredible.' He took a breath. 'And I'm sorry I hurt you this morning.'

'I'm not going to say it's OK.'

'I don't expect you to.'

With a sniff, she tilted her head and looked up at him. 'So what happens now? Jacob is back, Nathaniel. You can't change that and you can't run from the past for ever.'

'I'm *not* running. I just wasn't in the mood for the whole family reunion thing.'

'Surely the press must know about your father? Did you really manage to keep that quiet?'

'It gets dug up periodically. I'm hoping that a Sapphire win will make them bury it and focus on my career rather than my personal life.'

'That's why you want to win a Sapphire so badly? To distract the press?'

'It's one reason.' Nathaniel stood for a moment, staring towards the water. *He should tell her.* He should just tell her the rest of his story.

The sound of a helicopter cut through their conversation and she glanced up at the sky. 'Looks like your ride to Rio is here.'

'Our ride.' He stroked his fingers through her hair. 'You're coming with me.'

She pulled away from him. 'I don't think so. I'll be fine here.'

'I want you with me.' Just how much he wanted her with him shook him to the core. Jumping out of an aeroplane or scaling a sheer cliff face seemed less daunting than plunging into a relationship with Katie. 'You'll love Rio. It's the most exciting city in the world. Please.'

She rubbed her foot over the sand, drawing a pattern. 'If I came where would we stay?'

'We'll crash in Rafael's penthouse.'

'Who is Rafael?'

'Another half-brother. As you can see, I'm plagued by half-brothers, but they do come in handy when you want somewhere exclusive and private to stay.'

'Rafael?' She looked dazed. 'How many wives *did* your father have?'

'Four? No, I think it might have been three, but it gets confusing because of all the mistresses. Do those count?' Nathaniel slid his fingers through hers and they started to walk back along the beach. 'His bedroom was busier than Hollywood Boulevard on Sapphire night.'

'So is Rafael younger?'

'We're the same age. He's the son of the woman my father slept with while my mother was expecting me.'

She stopped walking. 'He—oh, my God. But you're close?'

'Close?' Nathaniel frowned at the question. 'I live in LA and he lives in Brazil. I have no idea how far that is. Ten thousand kilometres? More?'

'No, I mean—'

'Oh, you mean *close* as in brothers. That's a typically Katie question.' He didn't know whether to be amused or exasperated that she wanted everyone to bond. 'I use his place in Rio. He crashes at mine in LA If we happen to overlap, then we go and get drunk together. If you call that close, then we're close. Does that satisfy the rules of Katie-land?'

Her expression was serious. 'That must be a difficult relationship.'

'What's difficult about it?'

'Well, because—'

'Because my father slept with his mother? That wasn't Rafael's fault. He wasn't there.' Nathaniel gave a sardonic smile. 'At least, not until nine months afterwards. And now that's enough about my family. There's only so much reminiscing I can stand in one day and we're definitely into injury time.'

'So, will I meet Rafael?'

She was imagining happy family gatherings. 'No chance. We're going to Rio so that we can have steaming-hot sex in the land of the steaming-hot samba.'

'I've never even danced the samba.'

'Don't worry—' he flashed her a smile and took her hand as they walked along the beach '—I'm going to teach you. The way you move your hips, you'll be a natural.'

* * *

'This place is incredible.' Katie stared at the view from the terrace of the exclusive penthouse apartment. 'Your brother must be very successful.'

'He's slowly taking over the technology world.' Nathaniel leaned on the balcony and scanned the beach. 'Rafael and I have got drunk on this balcony more times than I want to remember. Whatever you do, don't touch anything. He's a techno genius and this whole place is run by gadgets. If you sneeze some piece of electrical equipment will probably hand you a tissue. I've told him that the day he invents an app for my phone that will kill photographers, I'll invest in his company.' He slid his hand behind her neck and brought his mouth down on hers and Katie gave a low moan.

All he had to do was kiss her and she melted every time.

She was a total pushover.

Disturbed by that thought, she eased away from him. Last night she'd given him everything. Today she was a little more cautious. 'Are we going sightseeing?'

'Of course. This is Rio.'

Nathaniel took her everywhere. They drank in the spectacular views from Pão de Açúcar, Sugarloaf Mountain, and ate in a beachside restaurant packed with locals.

When they arrived back at the apartment it was late and Katie automatically walked towards the bedroom but he closed his fingers around her wrist.

'Rio is just waking up. Tempted as I am at the thought of an early night—' his kiss was swift but devastating '—we're going to samba school.'

'School? It's almost midnight.'

'It isn't a school in the sense that you mean. The samba schools are part of the neighbourhood where people go to dance. Part of Rio's culture. They're all rehearsing for the Carnival in a few weeks' time. Here—' he picked up a box that had been delivered earlier '—I bought you something to wear.'

'You're in jeans.' Delving through layers of tissue paper, she retrieved a short dress in a vibrant shade of electric blue, dipping to the waist and ending in a flared skirt. 'I might as well go naked.'

'There's something else in the box.'

Katie shifted the tissue paper and found an emerald-green sequined bikini top. She blinked. 'Gosh. That's—'

'Perfect for dancing the samba.'

She hadn't worn brown since she'd arrived in South America. And that was because of Nathaniel. *He'd brought colour into her life.* Being with him had given her confidence. 'I love it.' Katie examined the flow and texture of the fabric and then disappeared into the bedroom to change.

Nathaniel followed her and she was conscious of him watching her as she pulled on the dress. 'Stop staring.'

'You have fantastic legs.'

'All the better for dancing.' She met his eyes in the mirror. *Felt the sharp stab of chemistry.* 'Shall we go?'

It was the most exciting evening of her life, although whether it was the dancing or just being with Nathaniel, she didn't know.

The samba was an innately sexual dance and Nathaniel was a hotly sexual man. Those heavy-lidded blue eyes and that slow, masculine smile soon drew the attention of every woman in the room—that and his enviable sense of rhythm and the effortless way he moved. He danced with a natural grace and an unapologetic sensuality that blurred the lines between bedroom and ballroom. Dancing with him was a hedonistic experience that was a full-on assault of her senses and Katie felt her head and her heart spin as their eyes held and their bodies touched.

Drowning in those blue eyes, Katie suddenly wanted to be alone with him. 'Can we go home?'

'You're not enjoying the samba, angel?' His smile was slow

and knowing and her heart was performing its own version of the samba.

'I love the samba.'

The heat flowing between them was immense and he curved a strong hand over her hip and held her against him for a moment. The lazy humour in his eyes turned sharp and hungry. 'You're right. Let's go.' He took her hand and virtually dragged her out of the building and into the waiting car.

The instant the doors closed, they were kissing and they kissed all the way back to the apartment, their mouths frantic, hot, explosive as they feasted. His hands were under the flirty skirt of her dress and Katie moaned and curved her leg over his, urging him on. She loved the way he watched her, with eyes half shut and the promise of ecstasy shimmering in the depths of that blue gaze. The excitement of his skilled touch was intensified a thousand times by that raw masculine sex appeal. All over the world, women had posters of him on their walls. Just looking at him was a visual pleasure but Katie tried not to dwell on that because she didn't want to think about him as a movie star. As a movie star he was unobtainable, out of her league. As a man—

They shared a fierce, explosive chemistry.

'We're here.' His voice thickened by passion, he lifted his head, his eyes still on her mouth. 'We need to take this inside or we'll be arrested. Two minutes,' he promised thickly. 'We just have to get ourselves up in that elevator and into the apartment.'

Trembling with anticipation, Katie followed him out of the car, too embarrassed to look at the driver. They were kissing as they tumbled into the lift that led to Rafael's luxurious penthouse, and then Nathaniel lifted her so that she straddled him and pressed her back hard against the mirrored wall.

'Two minutes is too long.' He groaned and Katie was so desperately excited after dancing with him that she simply sobbed her encouragement as he unzipped his jeans.

Caught in a vortex of excitement, she was blind to her surroundings, blind to everything except him. He was silken warmth and hard masculinity and then he was inside her and the delicious shock of it made her gasp.

'Oh, yes…' Her head tilted back against the cool, hard mirror as he thrust into her. It was hot and primal, as out of control as that first night in the tropical gardens of Wolfe Island.

A gentle ringing sound indicated that they'd reached the penthouse. Without lifting his mouth from hers, Nathaniel slammed his hand against the panel of buttons, trying to hit the one that stopped the lift. Instead he hit the one for the ground floor and the lift started moving again.

'How do you stop this thing?' His eyes fevered with lust, he lifted his head impatiently and tried to focus on the buttons but Katie took advantage of the sudden shift in his attention to move her hips. He gave a thickened groan and turned his head back to her. '*Don't* move. You're killing me….'

'I want—I need—' Her voice broke and his hands plunged into her hair and his mouth devoured hers in a hungry kiss.

'I have to stop this damned lift.'

He was deep inside her and she tried to match his rhythm but he held her trapped, controlling every movement, each virile thrust sending an explosion of sensation through her. Katie was sucked down into a world of dark, dangerous pleasure and she cried out his name and clung to his shoulders, feeling the strength and power under her fingers.

Breathing heavily, Nathaniel thumped his hand blindly against the lift buttons again and this time hit the stop button.

The lift jerked and then stopped and he gave an unsteady smile. '*Finally* I can concentrate….'

Somewhere in the distance Katie heard bells ringing but she wasn't given the opportunity to focus on it because he was turning their sexual encounter into a single-minded orgy of sensation. Pleasure slid through her in smooth waves and then rushed forward, building in pace as he drove them both higher and higher.

It was sex at its most basic, sheer self-indulgence, the slaking of the desperate hunger that consumed both of them.

'Watch us,' he ordered in a thickened tone, 'watch us in the mirror.'

Her eyelids felt heavy but she opened them, looking first at him and then over his shoulder. And watching intensified everything. Reflected in the mirror, she saw the contrast between her sun-warmed skin and his darker, hair-roughened thigh. Soft and hard. Tough and fragile. Male and female. It was his strength that held them in this position. His strength that drove them both forward towards the peak of pleasure. There was fire in her blood and a wildness burst from within her as sensation exploded through her body.

She cried out his name and he rode her hard, his eyes locked with hers, drawing every part of her into him. She felt him fill her completely, felt the male fullness of him as he thrust deep and she tore at his shirt, desperate to touch. Her heart was pounding, her breathing was shallow and uneven, and she clutched at the sleek muscle of his shoulders, feeling everything inside her fly free. Her climax hit like a lightning bolt and she tumbled over the edge into ecstasy, sobbing his name and holding tight as the explosion of passion took him with her.

It took a long time for everything to settle, for the world to return to normal.

Finally Nathaniel slowly lifted his mouth from hers. His eyes hazy and far from focused, he tilted his head. 'What's that awful noise?'

Katie struggled to breathe. 'I think the alarm went off when you hit the stop button. You're only supposed to press that button in an emergency.'

'That's fine, then—' with a wicked smile, he lowered

his mouth to hers again '—because it was definitely an emergency.'

She moaned against his mouth. 'I expect there are a team of engineers on the way or something.'

Nathaniel lifted his head reluctantly and slammed his hand against the lift button.

Katie made a strangled sound. 'Now we're going down instead of up.'

Tearing his eyes from hers, he looked at the buttons. 'Oops.'

He just had time to lower her to the floor and swiftly rearrange their clothing before the lift doors opened on the foyer.

Two of Rafael's security team stood there looking perplexed.

Scarlet faced, Katie wanted to slide to the floor with embarrassment but Nathaniel simply smiled. 'Having a good evening, guys?'

'Er, was there a problem, sir?'

'We had a slight malfunction, but I fixed it.' Adopting his customary bored tone, Nathaniel threw an intimate smile at Katie and once again pressed the button that took the lift straight to the penthouse. 'I'm good with my hands.'

As the door slid closed Katie sagged against the mirrored walls and covered her face. 'Why did you have to say that? They knew what we were doing. Just *don't* tell me there was CCTV in here.'

'Why? I can give you some insider tips if you like. The secret of performing in front of the camera is to act as though it isn't there. Although that definitely should have been a closed set.' Laughing at her, he swung her into his arms and took her onto the terrace. 'Where do you think? Day bed? Night bed? Floor? Wall? Shower? All of the above?'

Breathing in the sweet scent of exotic flowers, Katie stared up at his darkened jaw and felt ridiculously happy.

'You're insatiable.'

'Guilty as charged.' In the end he tumbled her onto the day bed on the terrace and proceeded to prove to her just how insatiable.

They fell asleep on the terrace and woke to the unforgettable sight of the sun rising over Sugarloaf Mountain.

Katie stared dreamily at the incredible view. 'This place is truly amazing.'

'Yes. Rafael has impeccable taste when it comes to real estate.' Nathaniel stifled a yawn and kissed her. 'Don't get up. I have some business to attend to today. I'll see you a bit later. Take a bath. Chill out.' With a reluctant sigh and a last look at her mouth, he sprang from the bed and picked up a stack of papers and a glossy report.

Still half asleep, Katie sat up. 'Business? What business?'

'Rafael and I sponsor a drama project here. Disadvantaged kids.' He hesitated and then dropped the report on her lap. 'It's full of heart-tugging stuff designed to make people with too much money part with some of it. I have to meet with the woman who runs it—it won't take long.'

With the hiss of the shower in the background, Katie flicked through the pages. Then she turned back to the beginning and read slowly. When she lifted her head, her face was wet with tears. 'The life some of these kids have led…'

Knotting a towel around his hips, Nathaniel frowned. 'Why are crying? You don't know them.'

'I'm crying because it's awful.' And because he was reaching out to children who'd suffered as he had suffered. Reading it made her think about what he must have experienced. Children in hell. *Was he even aware of what he was doing?* 'It must be so rewarding to be able to do this. To watch them develop.'

'I don't actually "watch them." I don't meet any of the kids.' Nathaniel thrust his arms into a fresh shirt. 'I just write the cheques.'

'You've never visited one of your projects?' Katie stared down at the report in her hands. 'Aren't you interested to see who these people are?'

'I know who they are.' He snatched his shorts from the chair, his tone brittle. 'They're kids. The idea is to try and keep them off the streets and out of the gangs. Being involved in these youth projects stops the kids picking up a gun. That's what the project does.'

'But you've never met them?' Katie slid out of bed and walked across to him. His hair was wet from the shower and flopped in dark spikes over his handsome face. 'Aren't you curious?'

'No.' The panic in his eyes was so swiftly veiled she wondered if she'd imagined it.

'It would mean a lot to them to see Nathaniel Wolfe in person.'

'I don't get personally involved.'

'So why help them?'

'Because I earn enough to give some of it away.'

He could have given his money to any number of charities, Katie mused, but he'd chosen to give it to children from difficult, violent backgrounds.

There was no way that was a coincidence.

She wondered if he was even aware of his reasons for championing that cause.

'If you showed up, the children would be thrilled.'

'And I care about that because…?'

'Because you care about helping the children. If you didn't care, you wouldn't be giving them money. You'd be giving the money to the cats' home or some other worthy charity.'

He reached for his watch. 'Maybe I'm the cold-hearted bastard they say I am.'

He wasn't. She knew he wasn't. But he wouldn't allow himself to become close to anyone. 'Cold-hearted bastards don't risk their lives rescuing drowning children. And they don't waste time and money sponsoring acting projects that the media don't even know about. You should go and see what they do. Imagine how that would make you feel.'

'Bored? I don't do things for other people.' He sank his hands into her hair and kissed her neck. 'I'm intrinsically selfish.'

'That's what you like to think about yourself, but it isn't true. Nathaniel…' She gave a low moan as his mouth found a sensitive spot. 'Don't. I can't think when you—oh…'

With a satisfied laugh, he tumbled her down onto the soft rug and it was another hour before either of them thought about moving.

'I could help with the costumes.' Katie curled herself around him, trailing her fingers down his body. 'I have all those ribbons and pieces of fabric I bought in the market yesterday. Who makes their costumes at the moment?'

'Don't you ever give up?' Nathaniel rolled her onto her back and looked at her, his blue eyes blazing in exasperation. 'I was going to get this meeting over with and then take you sightseeing.'

'I'd much rather help out at your acting project. Please, Nathaniel. You'll make their day. Their whole *year*.' The thought of what it would mean to the children excited her almost as much as what it could mean to him. She'd seen the compassion behind the tough exterior. She knew how much of himself he kept locked up. Maybe working with children would help unlock that part of himself.

Nathaniel swore fluently and sprang to his feet. His eyes menacing, he threw her a warning glance. 'Cry once, *just once*, and we're leaving. Understood?'

Nathaniel stood outside the building that housed his youth drama project, stomach churning. Any minute now he was going to be on his knees in the gutter, throwing up.

Why had he agreed to this?

Above them a chaotic maze of tin-roofed, wooden and unpainted brick shacks hung precariously from a steep hillside and wide-eyed, curious children watched them as they kicked a football in the dusty street.

The air was hot and sticky but Nathaniel had never felt colder.

He took a step backwards and then felt Katie's hand close over his.

'Let's go inside and meet some of them.'

Nathaniel wanted to pull away. He wanted to go inside about as much as he wanted to shoot himself in the head. He didn't want to get to know these people. He didn't want to find himself back there but Katie was pulling him and he couldn't find a reason to stay outside.

Inside the building a crowd of children of various heights and ages were milling around. The moment Nathaniel walked across the threshold the atmosphere changed. Everybody stopped talking and just stared. He was used to that, of course. It happened everywhere. But this was different. The eyes looking at him were different.

The silence lasted only seconds and then the room erupted into excited squeals and non-stop chatter as a crowd of children of various ages surged towards them.

Erecting the usual barriers between himself and the rest of the world, Nathaniel switched into actor mode and tried to distance himself.

But he wasn't able to distance himself. Unlike adults, the children didn't respect boundaries and soon several of the younger ones were climbing all over him, talking simultaneously, touching him to see if he was real.

He saw scuffed shoes and unwashed hair. He saw bruises and eyes that held stories no one wanted to hear. But most of all he saw enthusiasm and excitement. Yes, there was trauma there, but it came a poor second to hope.

The sickness inside him faded. His hands relaxed.

He signed a few autographs before remembering that he never signed autographs.

'Oi, tudo bem?' He spoke in Portuguese and Gabriela, a slim dark-haired woman who ran the centre, clapped her hands and commanded silence.

'We're overwhelmed that you have chosen to visit us in person.' There were tears in her eyes and Nathaniel tried to think of a slick, movie-star response but his tongue had tied itself in a knot and his acting cloak failed him, just as it had that night onstage.

'Show me what you're doing,' he said roughly. 'Maybe I—I can try and help.' *Great. Now he couldn't even string a sentence together.*

At first it felt awkward. Taking him to one side, Gabriela told him a little about each child and they acted scenes for him, proud to show off what they'd been doing. Some of them were wooden; others were better, and one or two had real talent. But it was the one boy who refused to join in who drew his attention. Watchful and tense, he stood close to the door.

'That kid over there—' Nathaniel wiped his forearm over his brow. 'What's his story?'

'I don't know.' Gabriela handed him water. 'He comes and watches sometimes. If you try and speak to him, he runs. I suspect he's just hiding out here. Best to leave him and hope that one day he'll have the confidence to join in. It happens sometimes. He isn't the first.'

Nathaniel looked at the boy and felt an immediate flash of recognition. In those eyes he saw defiance, anger, curiosity—*and fear.*

It was the fear that made Nathaniel stroll towards him.

The boy edged closer to the door and Nathaniel almost stopped walking. *What was he doing?* He didn't know anything about counselling kids. He didn't even know how old this one was. Ten? Older?

The boy turned his head, torn between the lure of the escape route and the lure of the world's most famous movie star. The movement revealed the livid bruise darkening one side of his jaw. His mouth tightening, Nathaniel kept walking. He didn't know anything about kids in general, but he knew about damaged kids. *Knew he was looking at one.*

Anger shot through him but he checked it as the boy glared at him, fists clenched. 'It's all right—I'm going. You don't have to throw me out.'

'Actually, I was hoping you could help me out….' Keeping what he hoped was a non-threatening distance, Nathaniel squatted down so that he was eye level with the boy. 'You're exactly right for this part—you ever act?'

The boy's fists relaxed slightly. 'I don't know anything about acting.'

'Good. It's easier that way than if you think you already know all there is to know.' Nathaniel held his gaze. 'So this is what you do—you forget all about being you, and pretend you're someone else. That's it. That's all there is to it. Easy.'

He was willing to bet the boy dreamed about being someone else almost every day of his life….

When a sheen of tears glazed the boy's eyes, Nathaniel didn't know which of them was more alarmed.

Out of his depth, he was about to call time and summon reinforcements in the form of Gabriela and Katie, when the boy grabbed his arm.

'I've seen your movies.'

Nathaniel felt a pressure behind his chest. 'Right. Good.'

'I— You've got plenty of actors here.' His voice was rough. Desperate. 'You don't need me.'

'Well, that shows how little you know.' Nathaniel saw the bruises on the boy's arms and the anger was a hard knot in his stomach. 'I need you really badly. So get your skinny butt on that stage and let's get to work.'

* * *

'No one has been able to persuade the boy to speak.' Gabriela was huddled with Katie, sewing costumes out of scraps of material. 'But now he's having an acting lesson with Nathaniel Wolfe. Katie, I just saw him *laugh.*'

'Don't. You'll set me off.' Katie blinked rapidly. 'I can't sew and cry.'

But Nathaniel's dogged determination to persuade the child to open up and participate had moved her. He'd refused to give up. Every time the boy had backed off, he'd been there, lowering his own barriers in order to help the child.

'Do you know how many times I've tried to get that boy to speak?' Gabriela threaded a needle. 'And now he has a part in the play. I have his name now—we can help him.'

Katie lifted her head and watched Nathaniel. He was demonstrating a movement to the children and they were watching, enraptured.

He would make a fantastic father.

The thought came out of nowhere and she froze, shocked by her own thoughts.

Oh, no, she wasn't going to do that, was she? She wasn't going to start thinking, even for a moment, that their relationship was more than a quick flash of fire.

Feeling a sharp pain, she looked down and realised she'd pierced her finger with the needle.

Katie grabbed a tissue and did a swift reality check.

Children? After his own scarred childhood?

Trying to distract herself, she sewed and produced costumes and made sure she was completely steady before she took a quick break and walked over to Nathaniel. 'You're doing well. I had no idea you spoke the language.'

'Rafael is Brazilian. We hung out together when we were younger.' He was watching two boys staging a fight scene, occasionally passing comment.

'Gabriela told me how much money you've ploughed into the project. She told me that you're the reason lots of those children are even alive today. How did you meet her?'

'Rafael sponsors education programmes—puts computers in schools, that sort of thing. He introduced me to Gabriela.' As the fight became rather too realistic, Nathaniel stepped forward and intervened. 'You're not actually supposed to beat each other. Do it like this—' He showed them how to make it look convincing without actually causing damage and then turned back to Katie. 'The whole thing snowballed. Sometimes our projects overlap. Two years ago Rafael sent me a script written by one of the kids he'd helped—it was good. We've turned it into a film.'

She was astonished. 'You found a studio to put up the money?'

'No.' His hand shot out and he steadied the boy before he fell and hit the floor. 'Rafael and I put up the money ourselves. It's a low-budget film, premiering at one of the film festivals in May. *Carnival*. Gritty urban thriller. It's about a boy from a violent family.' He turned his head, his eyes on Carlos, the boy he'd persuaded to join them. 'It's the life story of many of the kids here. Except in *Carnival*, acting gives the hero a chance at a new life.'

And he couldn't see the parallels? Acting had helped him escape from a difficult childhood and now he was offering the same escape to other children.

Katie swallowed. 'Who gave you that chance? Did you go to drama school?'

'Boarding school. My father couldn't wait to get rid of us all. I was happier at school than I was at home.' A frown touched his brows, as if that thought had only just occurred to him. 'The school had a fantastic drama department. When I was sixteen I was playing Romeo in a summer production. A Hollywood casting agent happened to be in the audience looking for an English teenager to play the lead in his coming-of-age blockbuster, *Summer Semester.* I was a complete unknown.'

'But talented.'

'I thought I was.' His smile was loaded with self-mockery. 'I just wanted to get the hell out of England. It was the ultimate teenage rebellion.'

He'd wanted to escape from the horrors of home.

'So you were swept off to Hollywood where you wowed everyone. What then?'

'I married my co-star.'

It felt as though something heavy had dropped on her chest. The noise around her faded and the only sound was her heart pounding in her ears. 'You...*married*?'

'You didn't know?'

'Why would I?'

'Because people generally like to study my life in minute detail and it isn't a secret. I thought you read celebrity magazines.'

'I just look at the pictures—to see what people are wearing.' *It didn't matter,* she told herself. It was in the past. It didn't have an impact on now. But it was just another example of why he was completely wrong for her. Information that she would have considered vital was locked away in the vault with restricted access. 'I—I didn't know you were married.'

He glanced at her. 'Now I see dark clouds in Katie-land. Why should the fact I've been married upset you?'

Because she'd stupidly fooled herself that he'd never been this close to a woman before. But he'd cared enough to marry someone. 'It doesn't upset me. I'm just a bit...surprised, that's all.'

'It was a publicity stunt. We were manipulated by the studio and the media—it was all about the movie.' There was a cynical edge to his voice. 'I never told her a thing about myself. In fact, I've never told any woman anything about myself, until I met you. You know more about me than anyone. If you're counting points, you're winning.'

'I'm not counting.' Katie's heart pounded. Or at least, she didn't want to be counting. All she knew was that something inside her had changed. That day on the boat when he'd saved the child—that night…

Her heart flipped.

It wasn't love. *Oh, no, no.* It couldn't be love. She wasn't going to let it be love. Not with this man.

Her stomach churned and she felt slightly sick. *How had it happened?* Less than two weeks ago she'd been going speed dating with Claire. She'd eaten cereal for every meal. She'd worn brown. Nathaniel Wolfe had been someone she'd fantasised about from a distance. And now…

She'd never considered herself to be reckless, but suddenly she was in love with a man who lived his life in the spotlight. A complicated man, all hard edges and armour plating.

A man who found it hard to talk about anything, least of all his emotions.

If that wasn't reckless, she didn't know what was.

They spent three days working with the kids on the acting project. Three days in which Nathaniel felt himself getting sucked deeper and deeper into the emotional issues he'd always made a point of avoiding. Part of him wanted to walk out and go back to the anonymity of writing big cheques. Instead he found himself talking to Gabriela, discussing ways in which the project could extend the support it offered for children. When a young boy revealed that his father beat him regularly Nathaniel ignored the cold slime that crawled over his skin and listened.

The older ones were harder to connect with. They'd learned to lock it away, *as he had.*

Any attempt to touch on the subject was met with resistance. 'So I've got secrets.' The shrug was years older than the boy. 'Don't you have secrets?'

Yes, he had secrets. He had secrets he carried with him every day of his life. The past churning inside him, Nathaniel turned his head to look at Katie.

Sensing his gaze, she looked up at him and smiled and the smile cut him like the blade of a razor because he knew there was still so much about him she didn't know.

What had she said to him? *I want to know the real Nathaniel.*

She'd barely scratched the surface.

As if to taunt him, he felt the phone in his pocket buzz with another message.

Even without checking, he knew who it was and knowing was enough to shake his mood from light to dark.

Normally when the black clouds descended he chose to do something reckless. A motorbike on a slick road. Free climbing a vertical cliff. Any raw physical challenge that required such concentration that nothing else could intrude.

Anything that helped him to forget…

Riding the anger and the stress, he strode across the room and grabbed Katie, pulling her into his arms. 'We're going.'

'But—'

'Don't argue.' Nathaniel spoke briefly to Gabriela, said goodbye to the children and surprised himself by promising to come back again really soon. Then he propelled Katie into the waiting car and drove straight to the airport.

'What are you doing?' Breathless, laughing, she moaned as his lips found hers.

Nathaniel was rough. Hungry. *Take me away from this. Make me forget.* 'I don't have a motorbike here and I don't feel like climbing a vertical cliff….'

Her eyes were smoky and soft. 'Is that supposed to mean something?'

'We're going back to Wolfe Island. I've had enough of sharing you.' He savoured her mouth, felt the punch of desire slam through his body, sought oblivion in the warm sweetness. 'I want you to myself.'

For the first time in his life he wasn't thinking of ways to end a relationship with a woman. In fact, he was looking for excuses to keep her with him.

He didn't want to share her with a bunch of children, however deserving.

Katie snuggled against him. 'And you think I'm going to argue with you? I love the island. And when it's just the two of us, you don't act. I get to see the real Nathaniel. No hiding. No secrets.'

No secrets.

Nathaniel felt cold fingers of guilt stroke his spine and the guilt angered him.

There was no reason why he had to tell her everything about himself. All right, so Katie had told him pretty much everything about herself, but that was her choice, wasn't it? Women were different like that. They liked to spill every thought and every feeling. Living like that would drive him mad. Most of his thoughts and feelings didn't bear thinking about, let alone repeating.

'So how long are we staying on the island?' She was smiling at him, unaware of the conflict of emotions at war inside him.

'Two days. Then I have to go back to LA for the Sapphire Award ceremony.'

She didn't say a word but he saw the brightness dim.

'And you're coming with me.' He didn't know he was going to say the words until they left his mouth. 'I want you to come with me.'

'To the Sapphires?' Her jaw dropped. 'You can't be serious.'

'I'm deadly serious.' Being with her felt good, he reasoned. She was easy company. Unselfish. Cheerful. And sexy.

Why wouldn't he want her with him?

It didn't mean anything.

CHAPTER EIGHT

It was all very well having good intentions. Harder to stick to them when the man you were determined not to fall for was Nathaniel Wolfe.

Katie curled up on the sofa in his private jet, trying to hold hope in check. It wasn't just the thought of attending the Sapphire ceremony that excited her, it was the knowledge that Nathaniel wanted her with him.

He could have flown her home or left her on the island.

But he'd chosen to invite her. Not a skinny A-list actress with visible hip bones. Her. Katie Field. Costume Designer.

And he was no longer acting when he was with her. He was the real Nathaniel.

'We've extended the acting project—' he was reading an email from Gabriela '—and she says Carlos has been back every day.'

'That's great.' And it was. But what really warmed her was how involved he'd become. Far from shutting himself off, he'd opened himself up.

'He's emailed me. Gabriela let him use the connection from her office.' His smile was tinged with self-mockery. 'I'm going to regret that one. Never given my private email to a snotty kid before. Next thing, he's going to want to come and stay with me in LA.' But there was satisfaction in his voice and a smile on his lips as he tapped a reply.

Katie blinked back the tears that stung her eyes. 'I think that would be great.'

Nathaniel turned his head slowly and held her gaze. 'I'm glad I got involved. I wouldn't have done it if it hadn't been for you.' He leaned forward and kissed her. They'd kissed so many times over the past two weeks, and yet this kiss was different. She felt the difference. And so did he.

Lifting his head, he frowned. 'Katie—'

She waited, her heart in her mouth. She had no idea what he wanted to say but she felt the tension and the shift in the atmosphere.

'Five minutes to landing.' The captain's voice filled the cabin and Nathaniel pulled back from her, his eyes blank.

'Nothing. We've arrived. Welcome to Los Angeles.'

They walked off the plane straight into a heaving crowd of reporters and photographers.

'Nathaniel? Is it true you saw your brother Jacob on your opening night in London?'

'Do you have any comment about why you walked off the stage?'

'Have you spoken to him since that night?'

Shocked by the relentless battering by the press, Katie gripped his hand, horrified that all the things he hated talking about were being flung out there for public consumption. To her it seemed monumentally insensitive and cruel and she wanted to shout at them to leave him alone but she knew that wouldn't help. They were like a pack of hungry hyenas converging on a juicy carcass. They showed respect for neither privacy nor personal space and she found the crowd and the cameras both threatening and intimidating.

The confidence she'd found on the island evaporated and suddenly she wanted to shrink into the background again.

In contrast, Nathaniel was cool and confident, striding through the ranks of photographers with a bored smile that was absolutely in character with his public persona. The man she'd spent the past two weeks with had vanished and he was every inch the remote, supersuccessful movie star.

'I have nothing to say about my private life,' he drawled, 'but if you want to talk about *Alpha Man*, then contact one of my team.'

'Do you blame Jacob for murdering your father?'

Nathaniel didn't break stride, nor did he give any indication that he'd heard, but Katie thought that he gripped her hand a little tighter.

'Do you think *Alpha Man* will win the Sapphire for Best Movie, Nathaniel?'

'Katie, how does it feel to have trapped the wealthiest movie star in the world? Is he paying off your debts?'

Before she had time to recover from the shock, Nathaniel sprang like a leopard trapping its prey. Lithe and lethal, he ploughed through the front row and grabbed the journalist by the front of his shirt, dragging him forward. 'She did not "trap" me,' he growled, 'and what I do with my money is none of your business.'

Frozen with shock, Katie closed her hand over his arm and tugged. 'Let him go. He isn't worth it.'

For a moment she thought he hadn't heard her, and then he released the journalist and the man staggered. His face was white and he looked shaken.

'Don't *ever* speak to her like that again or I'll rip your throat out.' Nathaniel wrapped a protective arm round Katie. 'Now leave us alone.'

Touched by his violent defence of her, Katie suddenly wished the journalists would just vanish. At that moment she felt closer to him than she ever had, and when he lowered his head to kiss her in blatant disregard of the cameras, she felt happiness brim over.

Through the mists of pleasure and the explosion of flash-bulbs she heard a voice—a clear, hard voice—shout from the back of the crowd. 'What about Carrie? Isn't it time you talked about Carrie?'

Because her mouth was pressed against his, she felt the change, felt the ripples of tension as he slowly lifted his head.

Anxious murmurings spread across the crowd from journalists worried that they'd missed an important story. People turned to one another, seeking enlightenment as to who 'Carrie' was.

The journalist who had spoken pushed to the front. She was an icy blonde who had ruthless ambition stamped over every centimetre of her carefully made-up face. Behind her was a cameraman determined not to miss a shot. 'Must have been a hell of a childhood, Nathaniel.'

Confused, Katie glanced at the woman and then back at Nathaniel. His face was the colour of the palest marble.

'My childhood was fine.'

'Really?' It was obvious that the journalist wasn't going to let it go. 'If I knew my mother tried to drown me when I was a baby, I don't think I'd be fine.'

His mother? Katie frowned, wondering how the woman could have got the story so wrong. It wasn't his mother who had tried to drown him, it was his father. She waited for Nathaniel to correct the woman but he stood silent, the black fury in his eyes sending an uneasy silence across the crowd of journalists.

The blonde took a step backwards but refused to abandon her story. 'You've been clever. You put out the story that your mother left, so none of us bothered looking. Why didn't you just tell people she had a complete breakdown and she's been in a psychiatric hospital ever since? You and your brother Sebastian should be proud that you used some of your many millions to build her a pretty cottage in the grounds so she thinks she's living a normal life. Why do you keep her a secret,

Nathaniel? Are you afraid that if people find out about your mother, it will ruin your perfect movie-star image?'

Carrie was his *mother*?

She was in a psychiatric hospital?

Katie's first impulse was to leap to his defence and deny it, but one look at Nathaniel's white face and traumatised expression told her that the woman was telling the truth.

And this time he didn't attack. He didn't move. It was as if he'd been felled at the knees.

And the warmth inside Katie melted in an instant. *His mother*, she thought numbly. Hauling back the sick disappointment that he hadn't told her, she focused on the blonde journalist. The woman's smile said everything. She knew she'd hit the jackpot.

Pushing her own pain aside, driven by a depth of anger she'd never known before, Katie stepped forward. 'How *dare* you use someone's personal life for cheap entertainment and to make a name for yourself. Shame on you.' Her voice shook and she stared at the woman with contempt. 'Shame on you.'

Shaking with anger, Katie stepped backwards just as six bulky men arrived and surrounded them.

'You're late,' Nathaniel said flatly, and the largest of the men gave him an apologetic look.

'Terrible traffic in downtown LA, boss. Sorry.'

They were ushered out to a waiting limousine and Katie collapsed into the luxurious interior. The warmth she'd felt when he'd leapt to her defence had seeped away through the stab wounds made by this latest discovery. *Why hadn't he told her?*

She glanced across at him but he sat in silence, withdrawn and remote. The Nathaniel she'd got to know on the island and in Rio—*the real Nathaniel*—was gone. Katie pushed aside her own pain. They'd only known each other for two weeks, she reasoned. For a man like him, that wasn't long enough to establish real trust. She needed to be patient. 'I'm sorry. She had no right to say all those things. How did she find out?'

Nathaniel tipped his head back against the seat and closed his eyes. 'The surprise isn't that she found out, but that it took everyone so long. Sebastian and I have been waiting for this for years. We tried to keep the secret—whenever there is press coverage about my father, it affects Carrie badly. She takes a lot of medication, but even with that, it isn't good.'

He didn't talk about it because he was trying to protect his mother. 'Why do you call her Carrie?'

'Because that's how I think of her. I stopped thinking of her as my mother a long time ago. She wasn't really capable of being a mother. She was too ill.'

'Is it true that you built her a cottage?'

'Sebastian and I wanted her to have as normal a life as possible. It's easier to keep her condition stable when she isn't around strangers. She lives in her own little world. Most of the time she's happy enough. She has full-time carers who she sees as family.'

'And what about you? Her real family?'

'I see her whenever I'm in England. But she doesn't recognise me. Or Sebastian.' Nathaniel's hands curled into fists. 'Do you know the really frustrating thing? She talks about me all the time. "My son Nathaniel, famous Hollywood movie star..." But she doesn't actually know it's me. She calls Sebastian "Nathaniel" but when I visit her, she can't seem to make the connection. Once she even asked me if I knew her son Nathaniel.'

Thinking about his bleak, loveless childhood brought a lump to her throat.

He'd learned to survive alone.

She slid along the seat and put her arms round him but he was rigid and unresponsive.

'I'm fine.'

'Nathaniel, you're not fine!'

'It's how it is. It's how it's always been. I need to warn the clinic.' Shrugging her away, he reached for his phone. 'They need to keep her away from newspapers and television. It could have a serious impact on her emotional stability. And then I need to increase security so those jackals can't get anywhere near her because she associates gangs of journalists with her disastrous marriage to my father. And the LA press don't have anything on the British tabloids.'

Katie sat there, helpless, trying not to feel hurt by his rejection. 'Are you going to call Sebastian?'

'I've just sent him a text.'

One by one the doors between him and the world were slamming shut. Katie wanted to put her foot in the final crack to stop him closing her out along with everyone else.

'You don't think a conversation might be helpful?'

'All he needs are the facts.'

Facts. Facts. Katie wanted to point out that there was more to conversation than an exchange of facts.

Picking up on her tension, Nathaniel turned his head and looked at her. 'You're upset that I didn't tell you—'

'No.' She pushed the words past stiff lips. 'It's how you cope with things. I understand.'

'Do you?' His voice was hard. 'Because if revelations about my family are going to shock you, then you're hanging out with the wrong guy. There are more skeletons in my family than in the average graveyard.' The brittle tone rubbed over her nerves like sandpaper and Katie tried desperately to regain some of the closeness they'd had on the island.

'I understand why you didn't tell me. I understand how much you must be hurting.'

'I'm not hurting.' The shield was up and no one was getting through. 'I stopped hurting twenty years ago.'

Katie stared at the perfect lines of his profile, despair seeping through her.

Not hurting?

He was in agony.

And she had no idea how to reach him.

'This place is incredible.' They were high up in the Hollywood Hills, near the urban wilderness of Runyon Canyon. Beneath them, the sprawl of Los Angeles lay in a haze of early-morning sunshine.

Sunbeams danced on the infinity pool and the place was infused with the delicious scent of pine.

'An architect friend of mine built it.' Distant and polite, Nathaniel poured her a cup of coffee. 'Down there is Sunset Boulevard.' He gestured with his head. 'And to the left you can see the high-rises of downtown. Did you sleep well?'

'Yes. Thank you.' *Did he really think she would have slept when he hadn't come to bed?* She wondered where he'd spent the night. Awake on the terrace thinking about his mother? Pacing?

Feeling utterly exhausted, Katie stared down at the city. It felt like a million miles from London in February. A million miles from her real life. Only her real life hadn't gone away, had it?

In the past twenty-four hours she'd come back down to earth and she was still bruised from the rough landing. 'I need to do something about finding a job.'

'Howard Kennington will be at the Sapphire ceremony tonight. You're going to meet him along with Alicia. There's a project they want to discuss with you.'

For a moment their problems receded into the background. Her head spun and excitement sparked inside her. '*The* Howard Kennington? The producer?'

'That's the one.

'But…how do you know the two of them will meet me?'

'I've already set it up.' Nathaniel was polite and formal and Katie felt as though her heart was being twisted in different directions. He was offering her a dream with one hand, while snatching back an entirely different dream with the other.

'Thank you,' she said quietly, 'for doing that for me.'

'I already sent your preliminary drawings and your costume plot. He's impressed and so is Alicia. The rest is up to you.' Nathaniel glanced at his watch, all brisk efficiency. 'You need to start getting ready for tonight.'

She hadn't even taken a sip of her coffee. 'Already?'

'This is the Sapphires.' He gave a sardonic smile. 'Most of the actresses started preparing at least two months ago.'

'You're kidding…' Awash with insecurities, she put her cup down on the table. 'Suddenly I'm not so excited about going—how do you fancy an evening in front of the TV?' Her feeble joke drew a flicker of a smile from him.

'Think of it this way—you're already at an advantage because you don't need Botox, plastic surgery, teeth-whitening or a month with a personal trainer. You're going to look fantastic and I predict much teeth gnashing among the glitterati.'

Panic set in. 'Nathaniel, I can't go to the Sapphires. For a start I don't have a dress.'

'Yes, you do. Follow me, Cinderella.' He walked across the terrace towards the house.

'I can't wear something you've chosen. There are loads of fabrics and colours I just don't look good in. And turquoise is fine for the beach, but it won't do for the Sapphires.' Wishing they were back on Wolfe Island where it was just the two of them, she followed him into the house. The vast windows threw sunshine and light over the polished wooden floors and elegant white furniture.

Silent and preoccupied, Nathaniel led her up the winding staircase to the master bedroom with its Brazilian wood balcony and views across the Santa Monica Mountains. But the last thing on her mind was the view.

Aware of the tension in him, Katie tried again to reach out to him. 'Nathaniel…about the press yesterday—'

'I have two well-known American designers waiting to talk to you if you don't like the dress.' Without giving her the chance to turn the conversation into something more personal, he gestured towards the dressing room that was about the same size as her apartment in London.

Walking into a room that dazzled with glass and mirrors, Katie blinked in shock. Hanging from a rail was the dress she'd designed. Her dress. It was taken straight from the drawing he'd admired that night in her flat, even down to the sequins hand stitched to the gold silk. 'Oh.' She swallowed. 'Nathaniel. How did you—? When did you—?'

'I found another drawing of it in your pad and sent it to a designer friend of mine. He's had a team of seamstresses working on it non-stop.'

'It's perfect. It's—' *An incredible gesture.* And she had no idea what to read into it. She'd never felt more confused in her life.

Nathaniel was watching her with an expression that she couldn't fathom. 'You approve?'

'How could I not?' Katie stepped forward, touching the fabric as she always did with any garment. 'It's exactly as I imagined it. Except that I didn't imagine I'd be wearing it myself.' Really touched, she flung her arms round his neck and hugged him. 'Thanks. That was incredibly thoughtful.'

It was like hugging a stone pillar—a one-way experience. There was no response. Nothing.

Nathaniel gently disengaged himself. 'I bought you something else….' His tone casual, he removed a box from his pocket and flipped it open. A beautiful diamond necklace winked at her from a bed of seductive black velvet.

'Oh—' Katie's heart stopped and suddenly she couldn't breathe. 'That's beautiful….'

And it was a breathtakingly extravagant gift. No one had ever given her anything that generous before. She stared at it, stunned.

'Pleased?'

'Of course.' And she was. It was crazy to think that what she really would have preferred was a hug. Or a kiss. Something intimate.

But Nathaniel made sure there was no opportunity for intimacy as he wheeled in a team of hairdressers, make-up artists and a top stylist.

By the middle of the afternoon, Katie had been primped and pampered and was feeling more and more nervous about the evening ahead. Why had she and Claire ever thought it would be fun going to the Sapphires? She was going to walk down that famous red carpet with some of the most beautiful women in the world on the arm of the sexiest man in the world. It didn't take a genius to predict what everyone would be thinking. *Why her?* It would be like letting a mongrel loose in a dog show, she thought gloomily. There was no way she'd ever win Best of Breed.

When she finally stepped into the dress, the stylist stood back and stared.

'You look totally awesome.'

Unconvinced, Katie turned to look in the mirror. And saw a stranger. They'd swept her hair up and the skilled use of make-up made her skin look flawless and her eyes huge.

'The dress is stunning.' The stylist sighed. 'Who is the designer?'

'Me.' Katie stared at her reflection, trying to see herself through the layers of sophistication. 'I'm the designer.'

'Wow. Well, by the end of the evening everyone will know who you are, that's for sure. I bet you're nervous. Every woman in the world is going to be watching that ceremony tonight and hating you for being with Nathaniel. Not to mention that several of the actresses attending tonight would have given just about anything to be in your position. He's a superstar.'

Nathaniel Wolfe, superstar.

Suddenly Katie wished they were back in Rio, helping

the kids with their drama class. There, Nathaniel had been himself. She'd started to get to know him, although there were huge parts of himself he still kept hidden.

Like why he wanted to win a Sapphire so badly.

She had a feeling it was more than personal pride.

Great actors went through their whole careers without winning, didn't they? Of course it would be a wonderful accolade, but was it really a matter of life or death?

She wondered if he'd talk about it on the way to the ceremony, but from the moment he strode into the room, she knew there was no hope of that.

There was no sign of the real Nathaniel. This was Alpha Man in person, impeccably dressed in a black tuxedo with a black satin bow tie at his throat. He exuded the raw, masculine glamour of the Hollywood leading man and Katie felt the gulf between them widen. It was like waking up from a wonderful dream and not being able to hold on to the images. She could feel him slipping away from her.

'Nathaniel…' Desperate to break through those barriers, she tried to talk to him but he was distant and unapproachable. She was no closer to him than those audiences watching him up on the big screen.

His fingers were cool as he fastened the diamonds around her neck. 'You look beautiful.' It was as if he was analysing her quality as another accessory to be fed into the whole Sapphire machinery.

'Nathaniel—'

'This evening must feel daunting.' Stepping back, he scanned her with those sexy, slanting eyes. 'You have no reason to be nervous. You will outshine everyone.'

'I love the necklace and I love the dress.' She wanted to tell him that it wasn't how she looked that worried her, it was how she felt. How *he* felt. The Nathaniel she'd fallen in love with had somehow slipped away when they'd landed in Los

Angeles. 'You must be feeling really nervous. I know tonight means a lot to you.'

'It's work. The Academy Awards are an important night in the calendar.' He was all movie star. Remote. Untouchable.

Katie caught his arm in a tight grip, trying to reach the man.

'*Please* tell me what's wrong. Is it just because you want to win so badly?'

'Of course I want to win.' His eyes burned brilliant blue. 'Winner takes all.'

Katie let her hand drop, wondering why she didn't believe him. 'So it's just your competitive nature.'

'We don't have time for a full-on Katie analysis session.' He held out his arm. 'The limo is waiting, as are the photographers. You might want to practise your smile.'

Katie hesitated and then took his arm and walked with him to the door. She'd been naïve, hadn't she? She'd congratulated herself on breaking down those barriers. She'd thought the man she'd spent the past two weeks with, the real Nathaniel Wolfe, was here to stay. She'd truly believed she had exclusive access, which showed how stupid she was.

It didn't matter what they'd shared. It didn't matter what had happened before.

Nathaniel Wolfe was gone.

It was a slow drive. The streets were closed off and people herded together and crushed against barriers, hoping to catch a glimpse of the stars. And then Katie found herself standing on the legendary red carpet, blinking in the blaze of the Californian sunshine. She touched the diamonds at her throat, listened to the screams and felt like a total impostor. It was controlled chaos, the sheer volume of people daunting, and she hoped that she didn't lose Nathaniel. She'd never find him again in this crowd.

A woman approached them, smiling and obsequious. 'Mr Wolfe, I'll walk you through. The cameras are waiting.'

Of course the cameras were waiting. *The cameras were always waiting for Nathaniel Wolfe.*

They headed along the red carpet and Katie spotted a sea of famous faces, but none as famous as Nathaniel, who engendered something close to hysteria in the watching crowds. They held banners and huge, blown-up photographs and yelled his name.

Calm and relaxed, he smiled and strolled as if he were walking on the beach, occasionally stopping to chat to someone or shake a hand. He was the megastar, the man everyone wanted to be or be with. Pushed into the reality of his world, Katie realised how hopeless it was. How had she ever thought, even for a moment, that this could work? Yes, she'd spent time with the real man, but he was also a movie star and that was never going to change. There would always be cameras and screaming women. Beautiful women. Drowning in a wash of despair, she walked through the metal detectors, trying not to tread on the glamorous dresses and embarrass herself.

And then she was being urged forward towards the banks of photographers and press desperate to interview the stars.

Katie wanted to shrink into the background but shrinking meant losing Nathaniel and his was the only face she knew so she stood and distracted herself by examining all the dresses and mentally altering the cut, the colour or the fit.

If her career as a costume designer hit the rocks, maybe she could become a stylist, she mused. She was good at dressing other people.

After endless photographs a voice announced that the awards ceremony would be starting in five minutes and Nathaniel guided her into their seats at the front of the auditorium.

Front row, she thought dizzily. *She was in the front row.*

As the Awards progressed, she felt Nathaniel's tension increase. The suspense was agonising and Katie sat there, heart pounding, unable to enjoy the evening because she was so desperate to get to the part that mattered for Nathaniel. She wanted him to win because she knew how badly *he* wanted it.

Even when she saw the words *Best Performance by an Actor in a Starring Role* flash onto the giant screen, it still wasn't over. Five beautiful actresses stood onstage to talk about each of the nominees and Katie held her breath thinking that if they didn't get on with it soon she was going to leap onstage and rip open the envelope herself. She ground her teeth as the women waxed lyrical about the other nominees, but when it came to Nathaniel's turn for acclaim, she found herself listening intently. As the beautiful actress, his co-star, started praising his raw talent, his intuition and his skill on both sides of the camera, Katie realised with a flash of guilt that she always tried to ignore that side of him. She tried to forget that he was a great actor because thinking of him like that simply intimidated her. But he was world-class. And clearly he had the respect of his peers.

Knowing that the cameras would be focused on him, Katie kept a fixed smile on her face, while the same thought revolved in her head, *Please let him win, please let him win.*

Finally the talking stopped.

The glamorous woman who had won Best Actress the previous year walked onto the stage.

Tense as a bow, Katie listened as the names of the nominees were read out again and then the actress finally opened the envelope. Her mouth curved into a smile as she looked up at the audience.

'And the Sapphire goes to Nathaniel Wolfe for *Alpha Man*.'

The applause exploded across the auditorium like a clap of thunder. Katie felt her vision blur and she turned to congratulate him, expecting to see him smiling. Instead he sat still, staring straight ahead.

'Nathaniel?' she choked out his name. 'You won. You did

it.' She gave him a little push and he turned to look at her, his eyes blank. 'Congratulations. They're waiting for you onstage. You have to go and get it!'

As he rose slowly to his feet, so did the audience. One by one, they stood, saluting him in an unprecedented show of support. There wasn't a person in the room who, by now, didn't know the sad story of his childhood. There wasn't a woman in the room who wasn't thinking about his mother as Nathaniel walked slowly towards the stage. The noise was deafening and there was no doubt in anyone's mind that it was a popular choice. Nathaniel could barely make it down the aisle for people hugging him, kissing him and shaking his hand. And Katie watched, pride lodged in her throat, tears stinging her eyes.

Eventually he extracted himself from the clinging hands and walked onto the stage to receive his Sapphire from Hollywood's hottest female star.

The applause was tumultuous, and in the midst of her happiness Katie felt a wash of despair.

For a while he'd been hers. Not Nathaniel Wolfe, Sapphire winner, but Nathaniel Wolfe the man. For a while they'd laughed, swum in the sea and made love. He'd shared his thoughts with her. He'd told her about his family. She knew that underneath those famous blue eyes was a caring, strong decent man who guarded his emotions.

But now…

Watching him lift the icicle shaped Sapphire trophy high in the air as a gesture of triumph, she felt her eyes sting.

He'd been a little boy trying to escape from the nightmare of the real world. And that little boy had fought his way to the top in the toughest business of all.

The achievement was outstanding.

When the applause died and the audience finally seated

themselves, Nathaniel gave his trademark sexy smile, back in control. 'This is the part where I'm supposed to cry, isn't it?'

Laughter rippled across the auditorium and Nathaniel spread his hands in mocking apology. 'Sorry to disappoint,' he drawled, 'but I've always had a problem with the crying part. Unless I'm being paid, of course. Thank you for this amazing honour....' He spoke fluently and with grace, thanking his co-star and all the people involved in the making of the film.

Then he paused and looked at the glittering trophy in his hand. Silence fell, as if everyone sensed that the obligatory thanks were over and that he was about to say something meaningful.

'I dedicate this Sapphire to my mother, Carrie.' His voice didn't waver and he spoke directly into the camera that was circling the front of the stage. 'Carrie, you are a beautiful, special woman and you always told me that one day your son Nathaniel was going to win a Sapphire. Well, you were right. I won. This is mine.' He held it high, a strange smile playing around his mouth. 'Maybe when you look at this on your mantelpiece, you'll think of me.'

Katie heard a quiet sob come from a woman in the row behind her. A man cleared his throat.

To the rest of the world it sounded like a simple dedication, but Katie understood the true message behind those words. Finally she understood what Nathaniel was trying to do.

He was hoping that seeing him holding the Sapphire would trigger something in his mother's brain. He was hoping it was going to be enough to make her remember that he was her son.

Tears poured down her cheeks and she brushed them away quickly, realising that the cameras might be on her.

Nathaniel left the stage to even louder applause and Katie

gave him a wobbly smile as he sat down next to her, expecting to see pride in his eyes. Instead his face had a greyish tinge and those famous blue eyes were empty.

'That was beautiful.' She covered his hand with hers. 'Will she be watching?'

'Yes. It's ridiculously late in England but she insists on watching the Sapphire ceremony every year. She even dresses up for it.'

A confused, lonely woman getting ready to watch the world-famous ceremony on a television.

Katie blinked rapidly. 'Well, you've made her night.'

He didn't respond and suddenly she wished they could just go home right now so that she could try and get him to talk to her. Instead they sat through the rest of the ceremony and then moved on to the Sapphire Ball.

Sparkling chandeliers sent a cascade of light over the decorated tables, the room a mixture of contemporary elegance and glamour. Nathaniel was immediately surrounded by people wanting to soak up his success and Katie found herself pushed back to the fringe of the group.

Wondering how anyone could feel invisible and conspicuous at the same time, she hovered. The falseness of the situation made her uncomfortable and she realised that this was why Nathaniel chose to hide himself. *You couldn't be real here, could you?* These people didn't want real—they wanted the dream.

She was wondering whether to pay an extended visit to the bathroom, when a man with a friendly smile approached.

'You must be Katie.' He extended his hand. 'Howard Kennington.'

Still worrying about Nathaniel, it took Katie a moment to register that she was in the presence of movie royalty. 'Oh…' She felt tense and awkward. 'Nathaniel said that he'd sent you my drawings, but—'

'They're awesome. As is that dress you're wearing. Even

Alicia is impressed and she's one hard nut to crack.' He drew her to one side and questioned her about her ideas and soon Katie was deep in conversation, talking non-stop as she spilled out a lifetime of dreams.

'Sorry.' Eventually she ground to a halt. 'I've gone on and on—'

'It's been most illuminating. You don't hide much, do you?'

'Nothing.' Katie turned scarlet. 'But I'm trying to change.'

'Don't. It makes you unique and it's hard to find anything unique in Tinseltown. You have real talent. As does Nathaniel.'

The famous producer smiled and they talked for another twenty minutes and when he gave her his card and invited her to meet both him and Alicia the following week, Katie felt her spirits soar. Howard Kennington liked her work. It was more than a dream. It was a fantasy. Never in a million years had she ever thought she'd have this sort of luck. It was all she could do not to squeal with joy.

If she could prove herself, she could be working as a costume designer on movies.

Virtually dancing across the floor, she went in search of Nathaniel, wanting to thank him and share her excitement.

She found him alone in a room used for press interviews.

He was sprawled on the red sofa, eyes closed. His bow tie dangled loose around his neck and his jacket was slung carelessly over the arm of a nearby chair. The coveted Sapphire lay at his feet on the floor.

'You look completely wrecked.' Deciding that this wasn't the time to tell him her good news, Katie walked over to him. 'Do you want to go home?'

'Are you kidding? The party is just getting started.' His eyes opened and she saw instantly that he was well on his way to being drunk. 'I won a Sapphire.'

'I know—'

'And with any luck, my mother might finally figure out who I am.' Decades of hurt shimmered in those words and Katie felt her heart break in two as she saw his mouth curve into the familiar mocking smile.

'Nathaniel—'

'Don't look at me with those big, sympathetic eyes. Life sucks, angel.' His eyes shone hard and cynical. 'You should know that by now. But you're still hoping, aren't you? You're still dreamy enough to be looking out for that happy ending.'

'I think sometimes you have to work on the happy ending.' She eyed the bottle of champagne that lay empty on the floor next to him.

Ever since his plane had touched down in LA, he'd been under the most enormous pressure. And then the emotional turmoil of winning the Sapphire…

'Your speech was—' she took a deep breath '—it was beautiful, Nathaniel. And I know how tough this whole thing must be for you.' Katie sat down next to him. 'Do you want to talk?'

'No. Absolutely not.' His eyes glittering like jewels, he slid his hand behind her head and pulled her mouth down to his. 'There are lots of things I want to do tonight, but talking is definitely *not* one of them.'

Katie tried to ignore the flash of sexual excitement. *No*, she thought desperately. Physically he was pulling her close, but emotionally he was pushing her away.

'Nathaniel—' she dragged her mouth from his '—you can't just run from this.'

'Do I look as though I'm running?' With a smooth, practised movement he shifted her under him and gave her a wicked smile. 'I'm lying. With you.'

'Yes, you're lying.' Desperate, she pushed at his chest, trying to ignore the way his body felt against hers. 'You're lying to yourself. You can't just pretend nothing is happening…'

'Nothing *is* happening—' he trailed his lips down her neck '—but it will in a minute. I'd better lock the door—I think this calls for a closed set....'

'No—' The chemistry threatened to suck her down. '*No*! This is crazy.'

'Sex with you is always crazy.' His mouth was warm and skilled and Katie turned her head away, trying desperately to ignore the pulsing excitement building inside her.

'You're doing what you always do in a crisis—you're acting.'

Slowly, he lifted his head. 'You think I'm acting?'

'Not the sex...' Her voice was husky. 'I think the sex is real. But it's the only thing that is. You can't keep running, Nathaniel—'

He said a word that shocked her and then he sprang to his feet and paced to the far side of the room. 'Why not?'

'Because it doesn't solve anything.' It would have been so easy to let the heat take her. *Take the easy route*, her body sang, tempting her. *Put your arms round him and do what you're aching to do.*

Nathaniel was staring at her, his eyes a dark, dangerous blue. 'I've had enough talking.'

'Have you returned Jacob's calls?'

'What business is it of yours?'

Katie flinched. 'None.' Anger mingled with the frustration. 'None at all. I can see that now.'

'Don't sulk.' He strolled towards her, his mouth flickering into that familiar slanting smile that made her dizzy. 'Tonight we're going to party.'

Her heart thudded, a slow unfamiliar beat in her chest. The anger glowed and burned. 'You can party. If how you feel is none of my business, then there's nothing more to be said.'

Bold dark brows met in a frown. 'Katie—'

'No.' She held up her hand. 'I don't want a relationship that's just about parties and glitter. I want a proper relationship, and if that means dealing with hard stuff, that's OK. I'm used to dealing with hard stuff. What I can't deal with is secrets. My dad had a whole secret life going on and I don't want to live like that. I *won't* live like that.' Outside the room she could hear laughter and cheers, but inside the room there was silence as Katie was forced to accept that he didn't actually care how she was feeling.

Nathaniel inhaled deeply. 'Katie Field…' A strange smile played around his mouth. 'Are you *dumping* me?'

'No. You're the one dumping me.' The anger burning red-hot, she stooped and picked up her bag. 'Face it, Nathaniel, you don't want a relationship. A relationship is about sharing—sharing the highs and the lows. And not just yours—everything isn't about you.' She swallowed. 'I came in here to tell you my news…I was excited—'

'You have something to celebrate?' He reached for another bottle of champagne and Katie felt her frustration boil over.

'Don't you think you've had enough?'

'I don't think so. In fact, I don't think I've had anywhere near enough.' He lifted the bottle and popped the cork. Foam spilled over his hand and dripped onto the floor.

Katie had never felt less like celebrating in her life. She felt cold. *Terribly cold.*

'You need to speak to Jacob,' she said. 'He's trying to make amends. That's obvious from the fact he keeps contacting you. You need to stop running. Be brave.'

'Brave?' His laugh was mocking. 'I'm Alpha Man and I have the Sapphire to prove it.'

Sadness spread like dark clouds, blotting out the final rays of happiness. 'That Sapphire just proves you're a brilliant actor. But I've always known that. You've been the actor, Nathaniel. Now you need to be the man.'

'You want me to prove I'm a man?'

'No.' Ignoring his slow, suggestive smile, Katie straightened her shoulders and held his gaze. 'Everyone thinks you're exactly like your character in *Alpha Man*, but you're not because he wasn't afraid to face his fears. You run from yours.' The dangerous glitter in his eyes made her wonder whether she should turn and run herself. Fast. 'I'm not talking about the physical stuff—you do all that easily because you're not afraid to take physical risks. I'm talking about the emotional stuff. That makes you feel vulnerable and you won't allow yourself to be vulnerable. You won't allow yourself to take emotional risks. Have you ever asked yourself why you take back-to-back roles with no break in between? It's because you don't want to leave a single chink in your schedule where you might actually have to be yourself. You don't even know who you really are because you've been hiding and running for so long. You won't go home because it reminds you of your past.' She discovered that her hands and knees were shaking. 'You avoid your family….'

His face lost its colour. 'My relationship with my family is none of your business.'

'You seem to think you're the only person in the world with a messy, difficult family, but you're not! Mine isn't exactly a picnic. We have our fair share of skeletons. I don't care. But I wanted to help you. I still want that. I love you…' She said the words without shame or hesitation. 'And I know that terrifies you but it's the truth. And when I think about what you lived through as a child it makes me boiling mad, Nathaniel, but what makes me even madder is that you're not prepared to face it and deal with it.'

A cynical gleam lit his eyes. 'And I thought you were such a sweet, sunny little thing. Clearly I had you all wrong.'

'Do you want to know what makes me most angry?'

'No—' he was icily polite '—but I'm sure you're about to tell me.'

'What makes me most angry is that you're prepared to destroy what we have because you're too cowardly to take a risk with your feelings. I know they hurt you, Nathaniel. Your father, Jacob—they all abandoned you. But are you really going to let the past dictate the way you live your life in the future? Before you can go forward, you have to go back. You have to talk to Jacob. You have to accept what happened and live with it, not just keep switching your phone off. You have to be who you really are.'

There was a long, pulsing silence. He watched her, his face inscrutable. 'Are you finished?'

Katie felt her heart crack in two. Hope drained away. The future, which a few hours earlier had seemed so bright, now seemed dark and empty. What they had was special. She knew that. *Why wouldn't he fight for it?* Why was he just giving up? Caught in a whirl of despair, misery and exasperation, she allowed herself a final long indulgent look at his face. *Memories*, she thought. That was all she was going to be left with. Desperately she imprinted images in her brain—the brilliant blue eyes, their astonishing colour intensified by the jet of his eyelashes and bold brows; the straight line of his nose and the slow curve of his sensual mouth. But the image that was going to stay with her for ever wasn't the movie star collecting his Sapphire, it was the man teaching disadvantaged children how to act. The man delving deep inside himself to help a vulnerable child.

Dredging up willpower she hadn't known she possessed, Katie lifted her chin. 'Yes—' her voice was shaky and sad '—I'm finished. And so are we.'

Feeling as though someone had gouged out her insides with a blunt instrument, she turned and stumbled through the door. Her vision swam and she narrowly avoided crashing into a group of people who were laughing together.

Blind, she kept ploughing forward until she ran smack into one of Nathaniel's security team.

'I'm not feeling well,' she choked. 'Mr Wolfe would like you to take me back to the apartment and then to the airport.'

She still had a credit card, didn't she? The fact that she'd never be able to pay it off was irrelevant. She'd book herself on the first flight into Heathrow and go home. She wasn't naïve enough to think that the Howard Kenningtons of this world would be interested in her if she wasn't with Nathaniel. It was all about who you know, wasn't it? Contacts.

Katie hurried down the steps. Like Cinderella, she thought, running from the ball. Except that she hadn't lost a shoe.

Both shoes were on her feet, but her heart was in pieces.

CHAPTER NINE

BEFORE you can go forward, you have to go back.

In a dangerous mood, Nathaniel floored the accelerator of his Ferrari and shot down the long drive that led to Wolfe Manor.

He'd swum with sharks, leaped from moving vehicles, sky-dived and climbed vertical cliffs but none of those activities had left him shaking the way he was shaking now. *Fear*, he thought. It lodged itself in his chest and gripped him by the throat.

What if, by going back, he was unable to move forward?

Centuries before, his ancestors had carefully planted an avenue of horse chestnut trees and they added an air of grandeur which was abruptly shattered as the main house came into view.

In a state of crumbling disrepair, Wolfe Manor stood like an ancient aristocrat struggling to maintain dignity in the face of advancing years and little maintenance.

Nathaniel killed the engine and sat for a moment, his fingers drumming a rhythm on the steering wheel.

What was he doing here? How did torturing himself with the past help solve the issues in his present?

Swearing under his breath, he sprang from the car and prowled through the tangled, long-neglected gardens. After the warmth of California, the bite of a British winter was particularly brutal and he turned up the collar of his jacket and blew clouds in the freezing air.

Afterwards, he realised that it had always been his intention to walk to the lake—*to confront that part of his past*—but now, as his feet moved, he felt as if he were being drawn there against his will.

He kicked his way through grass that was untended and overgrown. It brushed against his knees and wrapped itself around his ankles, impeding every step, as if warning him about the danger.

And then there it was.

Bulrushes clustered at the edge of the water, tall and straight as sentries as they guarded the dark, sinister pool that had dominated his childhood. It had begun here, he thought, and it had almost ended here, in the depths of the lake.

'You sank like a stone.'

His mind still trapped in another place, Nathaniel turned sharply to find Jacob watching him. Apart from that brief glimpse at the theatre, it had been almost twenty years since they'd laid eyes on each other and both had spent that time running. Isolating themselves from their past.

Nathaniel felt the anger rush down on him, vivid and scorching hot. The full force of twenty years of simmering resentment and pain powered the fist he slammed into Jacob's jaw. Pain exploded through his hand and Jacob staggered. But he didn't retaliate.

Nathaniel was shocked by how badly he wanted him to. *As if a good earthy physical pounding might right all the wrongs.*

Deep down he felt sick with himself because he knew the person he wanted to lay out cold had been dead for twenty years.

He stepped back. Let his hands fall. 'What the hell are you doing here?'

Jacob touched his fingers to his jaw, checking for damage. 'I thought it was time.'

'Why? Because we've all grown up?' Nathaniel heard the bitterness in his tone. 'We did it without you.'

There was a long silence, broken only by the ghostly howl of the bitter wind. 'Don't you ever pick up your phone?'

'Only when the caller is someone I want to speak to.'

'You have every right to be angry. I'm sorry about what happened at the theatre. I should have warned you I was coming.'

'Why did you come?'

'I wanted to see you.'

'Well, now you've seen me so you can leave.' His emotions in turmoil, Nathaniel turned to walk away but Jacob caught his arm.

'I'm not leaving. I'm here to stay.'

Nathaniel stood still, staring down at the hand that held his arm. Those hands had hauled him out of the lake and saved his life. Those hands had been responsible for the death of his father. Katie's words rang in his head. *He's trying to make amends—you need to stop running.*

Nathaniel scanned the rigid, forbidding lines of his half-brother's face and saw the same shadows that darkened his own life. And more. He saw pain and self-recrimination. Guilt and self-loathing. 'You look wrecked.'

'Thanks.' Jacob's laugh was devoid of humour. 'You look pretty rough yourself for a guy who's supposed to be the sexiest man on earth. Makes me wonder what the others look like.'

Despite the anger, Nathaniel's mouth curved into a reluctant smile. 'Ugly.'

'Too much post-Sapphire partying?'

Nathaniel didn't mention the fact that he'd skipped all the Sapphire parties to go after Katie. By the time he'd extracted himself from the hundreds of well-wishers and press, he'd arrived home to find the villa empty. She'd gone. Without telling him her news.

The emptiness in the pit of his stomach was something he'd never experienced before. This is what he did, wasn't it? He lived his life alone. He kept people at a distance.

If you don't care, you don't have anything to lose.

Jacob took a few steps forward, his eyes on the lake. 'What brought you back here?'

'Honestly? A woman accused me of being a coward so I thought I'd better just test the theory.' He blew clouds in the freezing air and Jacob gave a wry smile.

'You used to do that all the time when you were a kid. You pretended to be a dragon breathing fire. You were always entertaining us, pretending to be something. For you, it was a way out.'

'We did what we had to. You took up rugby to hide the bruises.'

Jacob's eyes were shadowed. 'Have you found a way to balance the make-believe with reality?'

Reality? *Reality was what he'd shared with Katie.*

And he'd walked away from it. Nathaniel stared at the glassy surface of the lake. No monsters, he thought. No ghosts. Just a dank, dark pool of water. 'I gave Carrie my Sapphire.'

'I heard your speech. Did she make the connection?'

Nathaniel was silent for a moment. 'I think she did. For a short time anyway. Or maybe that was just wishful thinking on my part.'

Jacob hesitated and then closed a hand over his shoulder. 'It was so hard for you and Sebastian.'

'Harder for Sebastian—she didn't even acknowledge his existence.'

'Whatever William may have told you, your mother loved you. When she took you into the water that night, she believed she was protecting you from our father. She was ill….'

Nathaniel stood rigid and unresponsive. It was the first time a member of his family had touched him since the night Jacob had walked out years before.

'Why didn't you hit me back?'

'Just now?' Jacob gave a crooked smile. 'Because I deserved it. Don't worry, I'm only allowing you the one. I thought you were going to leap off stage and punch me that night at the theatre.'

'I couldn't believe it when I saw you in the front row.'

'I wanted to see you. I should have let you know I was coming, but I suppose I was afraid you wouldn't want to see me. I was cowardly.'

'Seems we've all been guilty of that.'

'I left you all—' Jacob's voice was raw '—and you were just children. I don't blame you for hating me.'

Twenty years of pain and resentment melted away. Emotions left over from childhood suddenly seemed irrelevant. 'I don't hate you. You were hardly more than a child yourself.' It was what Katie had said, and suddenly Nathaniel knew it was true. He stood, thinking about how it must have been for Jacob. Just eighteen, with the death of his father on his conscience and no one to turn to, his only human contact a ragged bunch of out-of-control children. *Damaged, all of them.*

Nathaniel stared across the water, allowing his mind to drift back to that time. Katie was right. Those memories were part of the past. They had no place in the present.

'I was selfish.' The words came from deep inside him. 'I only thought about what it did to the family when you left. I only thought about us. Annabelle was distraught and watching her suffer made me feel as powerless as that night I watched William beat her. I didn't think about what it must have been like for you, living with what happened. We had you, but you had no one.'

'I shouldn't have left but at the time I couldn't see another way. I let you down.'

There was a tense moment and then they were embracing, holding each other tightly, the bonds of blood flowing from one to the other.

'When I saw you in the front row of the theatre that night, I had to warn Annabelle that you were back,' Nathaniel confessed in a raw tone. 'She was devastated when you left.' They eased apart, both of them awkward.

Clearing his throat, Jacob turned to look at Wolfe Manor. 'Did you know they've served me with a Dangerous Structure Notice for this place? Apparently I have to take urgent action to remove the danger, remedy the defects and carry out works to make the building and structure safe.' His laugh was edged with cynicism. 'It's hard to know where to begin. The roof is leaking, the brickwork is crumbling… We've had numerous break-ins. According to the police, local kids dare one another to sneak into the house.'

'The place was boarded up after we all left.' Nathaniel stared at the crumbling, forbidding house that had been the backdrop for the dark drama of his childhood. 'It feels strange, being back. It's been so long since I allowed myself to think of the place. I pretended it didn't exist. My whole childhood ceased to exist.'

'After I left, who stepped in?'

'Lucas.' Nathaniel kicked a stone into the water. 'Can you believe that? Naturally it wasn't a role he volunteered for. Lucas's idea of passing on fatherly advice was to teach us everything we ever needed to know about sex, how to avoid discipline and how to get drunk and still walk in a straight line. And—' he glanced at Jacob's jaw '—how to fight.'

'He taught you well.' With a rueful smile, Jacob ran a hand over his face. 'Although Lucas isn't the best role model for impressionable children. He slept with at least half of the girls in the school.'

'And a few of the teachers.'

Laughing, Jacob shook his head in despair. 'Do you see him?'

'Occasionally. He turned up late and drunk to one of my film premieres.' Nathaniel grinned at the memory. 'Staggered down the red carpet with some gorgeous blonde on his arm, winking at the paparazzi. I seem to remember the headlines were something like *Bad, Bad, Bad Brothers...*'

'Sounds like Lucas.'

'I bumped into him at Annabelle's Christmas party a few years ago. The one thing Lucas is good at is partying.'

'But none of you came back here?'

'Call me fussy,' Nathaniel drawled, 'but this place is lacking in party atmosphere.'

'It's full of memories.'

'Most of them bad ones.'

'Some. Perhaps it's time to make new ones. Remodel the place. Let in some light.'

'From what I've heard, you're the man to do that.' Nathaniel slid his hands into his pockets. 'I looked you up once. And Rafael mentioned that you've built a successful design business. You've done well.'

'And you. I haven't congratulated you on your Sapphire. I saw the film. You were incredible.'

For a moment Nathaniel thought about confessing how empty it all felt, how meaningless, but his tongue wouldn't form the words. What had Katie said? *Playing someone else is so easy for you, Nathaniel—it's being yourself that you find impossible.*

'Have you been inside the house?'

'Yes.' Jacob glanced at him. 'Do you want to take a look?'

They walked, and Nathaniel was surprised by how easy it was to be with his brother. Easier than being in the house.

Pushing open that heavy oak door, he shivered. *So many ghosts*, he thought. *So many secrets.*

'He's gone.' Jacob's voice was flat. 'William is gone. I was wrong to let the family drift apart, but I'm going to do something about that. Things are going to change, Nathaniel.'

'Maybe it's time for change.'

They paused at the foot of the grand staircase, now less than grand, each reliving private memories.

'You used to slide down this banister.' Jacob's mouth twitched as he ran his fingers over the cracked, neglected wood. 'It drove William nuts.'

'That's why I did it. Why did you leave when you did?'

'Guilt.'

'You saved Annabelle. Without you…' Nathaniel breathed deeply. 'Do you know how many times I blamed myself for not saving her?'

'You were nine years old. What could you have possibly done to protect her against a man like William?'

'Nothing.' Saying the word released something inside him. 'You stopped it. You were a hero.'

'Hero?' Jacob's mouth twisted. 'I don't think so. Annabelle was scarred for life. I should have prevented it happening in the first place.'

Nathaniel thought about William. 'He was unstoppable. You did what you had to do.'

'And I've lived with that every day of my life. The first time William hit me, I was six years old.' Jacob stared at a faded painting on the wall. 'He was drinking. I found him with a bottle of whisky in his hand. I didn't know what whisky was. I just knew it was a drink that made him angry, so I grabbed it out of his hand and poured it away. I thought that was it. I thought after that everything would be fine. I kept telling myself that. When you're a child you believe what you want to believe. And after he died—' The words hung in the air, the rest of the sentence unsaid. 'You say you blamed yourself for that night—there's nothing you can teach me about blame.'

Nathaniel realised just how much his brother was carrying. 'We weren't your responsibility.'

'Yes, you were. And I let you down. If I hadn't left, all of you might not be scattered around the world.'

'If you hadn't left, we might not be so successful,' Nathaniel drawled. 'Did you know Alex was the youngest driver to win the British Grand Prix at Silverstone?'

'I watched it on television while staying in one of Sebastian's hotels—the Singapore Grande Wolfe, I think.' Jacob stooped to pick up a broken photo frame that lay abandoned and forgotten on the dirty floor. He stared at the faded, cracked picture. 'We need to replace this with some of Annabelle's. Her work is astonishing. She finds beauty in everything. And then there's you—Sapphire-winning actor. Twenty million dollars for your last movie and a percentage of box office gross. What do you do with all that money?'

Nathaniel thought of the children in Rio and the projects he was exploring back in the U.S. 'I give it to Jack and he doubles it.'

'Yes, I gather he has rather a talent for investments.'

'And poker. Even Lucas refuses to play poker with him.'

'The tabloids have been full of stories about you and Katie Field. You're lucky finding someone who loves you like that.'

Feeling cold inside, Nathaniel concentrated on the graffiti sprayed on the wall. 'She walked out.'

'And you let her? Because you don't love her?'

'Because I *do* love her.' Acknowledging that for the first time, Nathaniel rubbed his fingers over his forehead, aware that Jacob was watching him.

'So you'd rather spend your life with women you don't care about?' His tone was heavy with irony. 'If there's logic there, I'm missing it.'

'If you don't care, you don't have anything to lose.'

'But you *do* care,' Jacob said quietly, 'and it's up to you to make sure you don't lose. Although I'm guessing it can't be easy for a woman, being with you.'

'Because I'm screwed up?'

'You're no more screwed up than anyone else. No, I was thinking about the publicity. Cameras in your face wherever you go. Women wanting to marry you and have your babies. On the other hand, maybe she likes all that.'

Nathaniel thought of the brown jumpers. The way she tried to blend into the background. Beautiful, caring Katie. On Wolfe Island, there had been nothing but the two of them. The crazy, insane Hollywood world had been nowhere in sight.

Nathaniel stared at the crumbling walls of Wolfe Manor, at the dust and the cracks. The history. Jacob would restore the house, he thought. Build a future from the rubble. *He needed to do the same thing.* 'She hates all that. She thinks I'm a different person in front of the camera.'

'Is she right?'

'Yes.' Nathaniel traced his initials in the dust. 'I've always hidden behind the acting. I didn't want to be myself. Maybe I was afraid of more rejection. If people reject the character you're playing it's not as personal as if they reject the real you.'

'You should be proud of who you are.' Jacob's voice was soft. 'You're an incredible actor. I've watched your career from the very start. You have a ferocious talent, Nathaniel. But you're also a good man. I know about all your charity work—about the drama projects for disadvantaged children. Rafael filled me in.'

'I just wrote cheques,' Nathaniel said gruffly, 'until Katie made me roll up my sleeves.' He thought about the children in Rio. 'This boy has been emailing me—I think he has real talent. I'm going to pay for him to go to drama school.' And others—it was a decision he'd made when he accepted his Sapphire. He wanted to give other children the chance he'd had.

'You've played a lot of roles. Now it's time to play yourself. With Katie. Go.' Jacob gave him a push. 'We'll get together another time. All of us. I'm back now and I'm staying. I have to stop this place from crumbling into the dirt and I intend to do the same for the rest of this family.'

Katie taped the lid of the last box. 'There.' She sat back on her heels and wiped her forehead with the sleeve of her jumper. *Keep busy. Keep busy.* 'I never knew I'd gathered so much stuff.'

'I can't believe you're packing boxes wearing a priceless necklace.' Claire put two mugs of tea down on the threadbare carpet.

'I'm just terrified I'll lose it.' Katie touched the diamonds at her throat. 'I haven't taken it off since I discovered I was still wearing it on the plane. I'll be relieved when it's finally gone.'

'Now you're talking rubbish. You'll be heartbroken when it's gone because it's the only thing you have of him.' Her voice gruff, Claire leaned forward and hugged her friend. 'You're so thin. I hate him for doing this to you.'

Terrified by how bad she felt, Katie pulled away. She'd never been in love before and she'd had no idea that it could hurt this much. The grief was huge and physical, a weight on her chest that she couldn't shift. 'Don't you dare cry or you'll start me off.'

'Sorry—I just can't believe you're going. What am I going to do without you? You're my best friend…you tell me what to wear.' Claire's eyes narrowed. 'I'm loving that red jumper, by the way. What happened to all your favourite shades of brown?'

Katie felt her eyes sting. 'I moved on,' she said huskily. 'Now, stop making me sad. You can come and stay. And we can email and text and there's always Skype and Facebook—' She broke off as someone hammered on her front door.

Claire looked at her watch. 'The removal men are early.'

'Katie?' Nathaniel's voice bellowed through the closed door. 'Open this damn door!'

Claire shot to her feet, tea sloshing onto the carpet. 'It's him! What's he doing here?'

Katie put her tea down carefully. 'He's here for his diamonds. I should have texted him to tell him I was planning to return it.'

'I don't think men like Nathaniel would bother travelling to another continent just to retrieve lost property.'

'Well, there isn't any other reason for him to be here.' Feeling sick and dizzy, Katie stood and smoothed her jumper. She didn't want to face him. She just wasn't sure she could hang on to control. Wishing she'd couriered the necklace back to him, she walked to the door and pulled it open.

Nathaniel stood there dressed in black leather, a motorbike helmet tucked under his arm.

Her knees went weak.

How was she going to cope? How could she forget about him when Nathaniel Wolfe's insanely handsome face stared back at her from every billboard and every magazine?

'Hi, I know why you're here.' She must have learned something from him, she thought, because it was only acting skills that kept her afloat. 'You've come for your property.'

'That's right.' His voice was smooth and sure and he glanced over her shoulder and saw Claire. 'Hi, Claire.'

Claire looked as though she might faint. 'You know my name….'

Katie put her hands behind her neck and unfastened the necklace. The diamonds seemed to symbolise all the reasons why this would never have worked. 'Here—' She held it out to him and he stared at it.

'Why are you giving me that?'

'You've come for your property.'

'That's right. But I don't want the necklace.' He studied her with those blue eyes that made women forget how to think straight and walk straight. 'I want you.'

There was a whimper and a thud behind her, but Katie was too busy keeping her own emotions under control to have any thoughts to spare for her friend. She wasn't going to fall for it. Yes, it sounded sincere. He was an actor. He earned a living making the unbelievable, believable. 'Take the necklace…' She pushed it into his hand. 'Get on with your life.' *Get out of my house before I make a complete fool of myself….*

'You have every right to be angry with me.' Without waiting for invitation, Nathaniel walked into the flat and kicked the door shut behind him.

Panic fluttered in her chest. 'What do you think you're doing?'

'You're always saying that if there's a problem, it's better to talk, so we're going to talk.'

Katie stood, mute, terrified to open her mouth in case this was the moment when she broke down and sobbed.

Nathaniel lifted an eyebrow. 'I'm giving you permission to talk—to say everything that's in your head.'

Katie said nothing.

'I think I'll just go for a walk.' Claire's voice was falsely bright. 'This is one scene where you definitely don't need any extras.' Grabbing her coat, she melted out of the flat, shutting the door firmly behind her.

Nathaniel didn't shift his gaze from Katie. 'This isn't like you.' When she still didn't answer, he gave an exasperated sigh. 'All right, maybe this time I'll do the talking. I went back to Wolfe Manor. I saw Jacob.'

Katie still said nothing, but her legs felt unsteady and everything inside her was churning.

'I went to the lake.' Something flickered in his eyes. 'I told you that William tried to drown me there—what I didn't tell you was that Carrie did the same thing when I was a baby. She'd just discovered that my father had produced a child with another woman. She was always emotionally fragile, but that night—well, it tipped her over the edge. Apparently she thought she was saving me.'

This time she found her voice. 'Nathaniel—'

'Are those your pictures of me?' He stared at the pile of magazines that she'd stacked by the door. 'Are you clearing them out of your life?'

'Never mind that.' She felt dizzy. 'Who saved you that night? When your mother walked into the lake with you?'

'Jacob and Lucas were home from the school holidays and were camping in the grounds. They waded in and rescued us both. Much to my father's fury—he beat them both for saving his "mad wife" and her unwanted child. That's me by the way.' His mouth twisted. 'I was the unwanted child. Apparently the only time my father was nice to my mother was when she was pregnant with my brother Sebastian. Unfortunately she made the mistake of thinking that history would repeat itself so she got herself pregnant again. *Big* mistake.'

Katie wrapped her arms around herself. 'Did she recognise you when you gave her the Sapphire?'

'I don't know.' His voice was soft. 'I think so but maybe that's just wishful thinking.'

'How is she?'

'Stable. On buckets of medication, of course, but happy enough in her own world. All we can do for her is protect her as much as we can.'

But it wasn't the child's job to protect the parent, was it?

Katie thought about her own childhood. Her father's hidden life didn't change the fact that she'd been loved. *Really loved.* 'I don't know how you survived.'

'I survived by becoming someone else. I acted my way through the most difficult years.' Nathaniel held her gaze. 'I was someone else pretty much the whole time until I met you. You're the first woman who has been interested in the man, not the movie star. The drama project in Rio—I just wanted to give money. I didn't want to know where it went. I didn't want to hear their stories. Maybe I was trying to get rid of the guilt I felt about not protecting Annabelle. If I helped some other child…' He gave a careless shrug. 'And then you suggested I get involved. And it changed everything.'

'Nathaniel—'

'I don't do "involved." I don't get down and dirty with people's emotions—I'm not good with all that stuff. But those kids were—' He frowned. 'I thought I was the one helping them, but it turned out they were the ones helping me. Watching them made me realise that you cannot let yourself be defined by what went before. It's never too late to build a new life. To do something different. To *want* something different. And I want something different, Katie. I don't want to wake up every morning and act my way through the day. I want to live *my* life, not someone else's.' His gaze burned into hers. 'And I want to live it with you.'

Her heart tried to fly but her brain wouldn't let it. *Don't be a fool, Katie.*

Nathaniel gave a crooked smile. 'Say something.'

'You won a Sapphire—' her voice was a croak '—you're the world's hottest movie star….'

'That's just my job—' he took her face in his hands, stroking her cheeks with his thumbs '—that's not who I am. You taught me that. You're the only person who ever cared enough to look past the performance. The only person who ever wanted to know me. And I want to carry on being me, with you by my side. I love you.' When she still didn't speak, his smile faltered. 'That's the first time I've ever said those words outside a film set.'

Still Katie kept the excitement tightly leashed. 'This is all very sudden—and unexpected….' She wasn't brave enough, was she? She wasn't brave enough to believe him. 'When did you decide that you loved me?'

'When I won a Sapphire and it meant nothing to me.' His

eyes raked her face, searching. 'I wanted to win it for Carrie, but the moment you walked out that night, I knew I hadn't won at all. I'd lost.'

'Nathaniel—'

'I know you think I'm a coward—' he lowered his forehead to hers, his voice unsteady '—but give me the chance to prove to you that I'm not. I'm a tough guy. Want to feel my muscles?'

The tears came then. They brimmed in her eyes and then slid past her smile. 'I know you're not a coward. I just wanted to make it better and you kept pushing me away.'

'I won't be doing that again. *Don't* cry. Please don't cry.' Nathaniel swiped the tears away from her cheeks and took her mouth in a brief, desperate kiss. 'Katie, I really— Please...I'm telling you I love you—say something.'

Terror and hope danced together. 'I can't let myself believe you. I don't know if you're acting.'

'You know I'm not acting. I love you and I want to spend the rest of my life living with you in Katie-land. And you can throw out those magazines because you have the real thing.'

She made a sound that was half laugh, half sob. 'We're so different....'

'Not so different. You hid behind brown clothes. I hid behind my job.'

'I haven't worn brown since Wolfe Island.' She sniffed and mopped her tears on the sleeve of her sweater. 'You made me feel beautiful.'

'You *are* beautiful.' Sliding his arms around her, he frowned. 'Have you lost weight?'

'I've been miserable.'

With a groan of remorse, he flattened her against him. 'I'm never letting you out of my sight again. I'm going to take you straight back to LA—'

'I'm already going back to LA' Katie pulled away from him and looked at the boxes stacked by the door. 'I spoke to Howard Kennington this week and he wants me to come out and work on his next movie. He really liked my work. I assumed it was because of you, but he was really cross that I'd flown back here without talking to him first. He sent me a flight ticket.'

'You won't be needing it because I'm going to fly you home. I knew your work was exceptional the moment I saw it.' He stroked her hair away from her face. 'I'm going to give up acting and concentrate on directing. We can work on films together.'

Together. Her heart twisted with emotion.

'Katie Field, Costume Designer.'

'Katie *Wolfe*, Costume Designer.'

She didn't dare move for fear of breaking the spell. 'Nathaniel—'

'I want you to marry me. Say you'll marry me.'

There was a buzzing in her ears. 'You want to *marry* me? But…you— Oh, my God—you'd break a billion female hearts.'

'There's only one female heart I care about,' he said softly, and cursed lightly as her eyes filled again. 'Don't do that. I can't stand it when you cry—I never want to see you cry ever again.'

'This time it's happy crying.' Katie leaned her head against his chest. 'I can't believe this….'

'Usually when I ask a woman to marry me I already know the answer because it's in the script.' Uncharacteristically unsure of himself, Nathaniel gave a horrified groan. 'I forgot the ring.' He swore under his breath and delved into his pocket. 'I'm doing this all wrong. I had it all planned out, the whole on-the-knee thing, fairy tale, Katie-land style, and then I saw you and—sorry, I'm sorry, can we do another take?' He dropped to his knees. 'Katie Field, will you marry me? Will you love me and talk to me as long as we both shall live?'

Her laughter turned to a gasp as he slid a huge, glittering diamond onto her finger. 'Oh, my—'

'If you don't like it we can choose a different one. Maybe I should have let you choose it. I'm sorry—as proposals go I totally messed that one up.'

'No, you didn't…' She could hardly make her voice work. 'It was perfect.'

'I forgot the ring and I forgot to go down on one knee,' he said dryly. 'What was perfect about it?'

'It was perfect because it was real. It came from the heart, not from a script. If you'd been fluent I would have thought you were acting.'

'Really?' His voice was raw and there was uncertainty in his eyes as he looked at her. 'In that case is there any chance of an answer some time this century?'

'Yes!' The word flew from her heart to her lips. 'Of course yes. I love you. You *know* I love you.'

Nathaniel rose to his feet and this time his kiss was hard and possessive. When he finally tore his mouth from hers, her head was spinning. 'Now you're wearing the ring and you can't back out, I need to break the news about my family. If you're hoping for conventional, then you might want to re-think. Jacob is determined to bring us all together so you'll be meeting them all over the next few months and you're going to wonder what you've got yourself involved in.'

'So will you…' Katie wrapped her arms around his neck, unable to contain the happiness that bubbled up inside her. 'There's something I haven't told you about myself.'

'*You've* been keeping secrets?' He started to laugh. 'You hypocrite—'

'Paula Preston is my sister.'

'Paula Preston?' He frowned. 'The supermodel?'

A horrible thought entered her head. 'Have you—? Did you ever—?'

'No. I definitely haven't. She's not my type. I assume she's the reason you wear brown and are a late developer.'

Katie bit her lip. 'It wasn't easy having her as a sister.'

'I can imagine. I met her once. Utter nightmare. But it's good to know I'm not the only one with colourful relatives. I think our wedding is going to be interesting.'

'You still want to marry me?'

'Of course. Why wouldn't I?'

'Paula is the beautiful one. People always make comparisons.'

He hauled her against him. 'There is no comparison. You're sweet, she's not. You care about people, she walks over people. And the biggest difference of all—' his smile was slow and sexy '—is your bottom. She doesn't have one and yours is every man's erotic fantasy. Want me to prove it?'

Katie blushed. 'If she comes to our wedding, she'll probably try and seduce you. None of your relatives can possibly be as embarrassing as my sister.'

'Don't you believe it. My brother Lucas doesn't think there's any point in going to a wedding if he can't try and have sex with the bride,' Nathaniel drawled. 'He will definitely try to seduce you at our wedding. Women love him, but I warn you that if you cast one look in his direction you'll be spending the rest of your life on Wolfe Island with just me for company.'

Katie slid her arms around his neck, feeling as if she were floating. 'An exotic island and the sexiest guy in the world? That sounds like a perfect ending to me.'

'In that case—' a smile touched the corners of his mouth and he lowered his head to kiss her '—it's a wrap.'

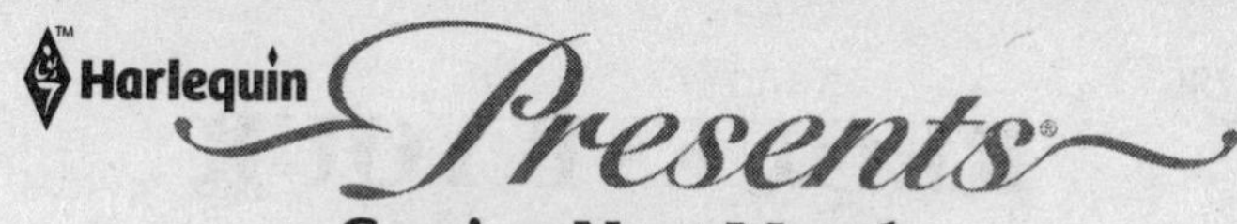

Coming Next Month

from **Harlequin Presents® EXTRA.** Available July 12, 2011

#157 A SPANISH AWAKENING
Kim Lawrence
One Night in...

#158 RECKLESS NIGHT IN RIO
Jennie Lucas
One Night in...

#159 THE END OF FAKING IT
Natalie Anderson
His Very Personal Assistant

#160 HER NOT-SO-SECRET DIARY
Anne Oliver
His Very Personal Assistant

Coming Next Month

from **Harlequin Presents®.** Available July 26, 2011

#3005 THE MARRIAGE BETRAYAL
Lynne Graham
The Volakis Vow

#3006 THE DISGRACED PLAYBOY
Caitlin Crews
The Notorious Wolfes

#3007 A DARK SICILIAN SECRET
Jane Porter

#3008 THE MATCHMAKER BRIDE
Kate Hewitt
The Powerful and the Pure

#3009 THE UNTAMED ARGENTINEAN
Susan Stephens

#3010 PRINCE OF SCANDAL
Annie West

Visit www.HarlequinInsideRomance.com
for more information on upcoming titles!

HPCNM0711

Once bitten, twice shy. That's Gabby Wade's motto—especially when it comes to Adamson men. And the moment she meets Jon Adamson her theory is confirmed. But with each encounter a little something *sparks between them, making her wonder if she's been too hasty to dismiss this one!*

Enjoy this sneak peek from ONE GOOD REASON by Sarah Mayberry, available August 2011 from Harlequin® Superromance®.

Gabby Wade's heartbeat thumped in her ears as she marched to her office. She wanted to pretend it was because of her brisk pace returning from the file room, but she wasn't that good a liar.

Her heart was beating like a tom-tom because Jon Adamson had touched her. In a very male, very possessive way. She could still feel the heat of his big hand burning through the seat of her khakis as he'd steadied her on the ladder.

It had taken every ounce of self-control to tell him to unhand her. What she'd really wanted was to grab him by his shirt and, well, explore all those urges his touch had instantly brought to life.

While she might not like him, she was wise enough to understand that it wasn't always about liking the other person. Sometimes it was about pure animal attraction.

Refusing to think about it, she turned to work. When she'd typed in the wrong figures three times, Gabby admitted she was too tired and too distracted. Time to call it a day.

As she was leaving, she spied Jon at his workbench in the shop. His head was propped on his hand as he studied blueprints. It wasn't until she got closer that she saw his eyes were shut.

He looked oddly boyish. There was something innocent and unguarded in his expression. She felt a weakening in her resistance to him.

"Jon." She put her hand on his shoulder, intending to shake him awake. Instead, it rested there like a caress.

His eyes snapped open.

"You were asleep."

"No, I was, uh, visualizing something on this design." He gestured to the blueprint in front of him then rubbed his eyes.

That gesture dealt a bigger blow to her resistance. She realized it wasn't only animal attraction pulling them together. She took a step backward as if to get away from the knowledge.

She cleared her throat. "I'm heading off now."

He gave her a smile, and she could see his exhaustion.

"Yeah, I should, too." He stood and stretched. The hem of his T-shirt rose as he arched his back and she caught a flash of hard male belly. She looked away, but it was too late. Her mind had committed the image to permanent memory.

And suddenly she knew, for good or bad, she'd never look at Jon the same way again.

Find out what happens next in ONE GOOD REASON, available August 2011 from Harlequin® Superromance®!

HSREXP0811

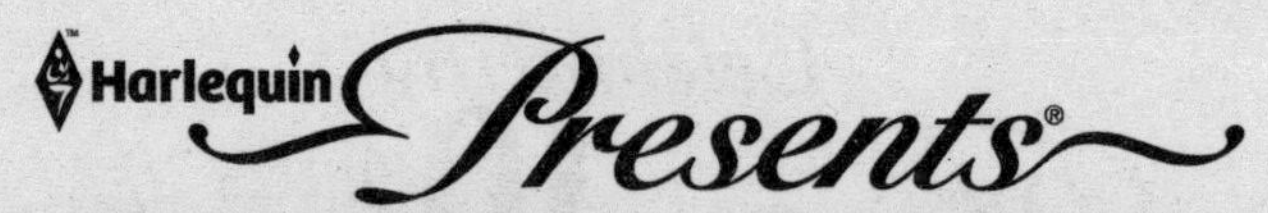

USA TODAY *bestselling author*

Lynne Graham

introduces her new Epic Duet

THE VOLAKIS VOW

A marriage made of secrets…

Tally Spencer, an ordinary girl with no experience of relationships… Sander Volakis, an impossibly rich and handsome Greek entrepreneur. Sander is expecting to love her and leave her, but for Tally this is love at first sight. Little does he know that Tally is expecting his baby…and blackmailing him to marry her!

PART ONE:
THE MARRIAGE BETRAYAL
Available August 2011

PART TWO:
BRIDE FOR REAL
Available September 2011

Available only from Harlequin Presents®.